"You continually amaze me, Cait Monahan," he said. "How many sides of you are there?"

His thumb traveled the length of her jaw, trailing down her slender neck. Her pulse leaped crazily, and she felt his fingers slide behind her neck and pull her toward him. Automatically she closed her eyes, her lips yielding as his mouth lightly touched her own. A flame leaped to life within her. A moan of pleasure rose in her throat as his tongue forced entry into her mouth, and her breath was suspended as a vortex of fire uncoiled within her quivering body.

He dragged his mouth from her lips, his eyes burning with a fierce light of desire.

"What are you doing to me?" he demanded rawly.

Dear Reader,

Your enthusiastic reception of SECOND CHANCE AT LOVE has inspired all of us who work on this special romance line and we thank you.

Now there are *six* brand new, exciting SECOND CHANCE AT LOVE romances for you each month. We've doubled the number of love stories in our line because so many readers like you asked us to. So, you see, your opinions, your ideas, what you think, really count! Feel free to drop me a note to let me know your reactions to our stories.

Again, thanks for so warmly welcoming SECOND CHANCE AT LOVE and, please, *do* let me hear from *you*!

With every good wish,

Carolyn Nichols

Carolyn Nichols
SECOND CHANCE AT LOVE
The Berkley/Jove Publishing Group
200 Madison Avenue
New York, New York 10016

HOLD FAST 'TIL MORNING
BETH BROOKES

A SECOND CHANCE AT LOVE BOOK

To Genivieve Nauman,
who loved romantic stories
as much as I do.

Chapter One

CAIT MONAHAN'S TRAVEL-WEARY eyes met the golden-brown gaze of the man striding like a caged jaguar next to the small flight desk. He gave a cursory glance to her dark hair, unbound and cascading like shining silk over her shoulders, and traveled down the length of her two-piece tweed pants suit. A shiver of awareness made Cait's skin tingle. From the way he was looking at her, you'd think he'd never seen a woman in slacks before. She shrugged with more nonchalance than she felt. Where she was going, jeans, shirts and hard hats were the usual attire.

The set of the man's mouth was grim and he moved noiselessly, each stride fluid, his bare arms powerful. He was dressed in jeans, a short-sleeved chambray shirt and rough work-boots. His clothes, although faded and well worn, accentuated his well-muscled male body. His thick brows were drawn downward in silent concentration, and his square face suggested a primitiveness barely held in check.

Cait's senses reeled with assorted impressions as his features changed like quicksilver. One moment he looked savage, the next merely deep in thought. She glanced behind the desk at the attendant, who was busy typing out a message, then turned to the restless stranger.

"Excuse me, is this the Miron Corporation flight desk?" she asked.

His insolent glance burned into her, and Cait stiffened. "Yes, it is," came the throaty reply. He gave her a look of exasperation, as if not wanting to be bothered by her presence. "Señora, you're obviously lost." His piercing gaze softened as he looked her up and down in slow appraisal. "However," he murmured, "your plight is a definite advantage to me. Beautiful women should never travel alone."

Cait stared wide-eyed at him, caught off guard by his sudden change in mood. His voice had spun a silken cocoon, like fingers stroking her skin, making her excruciatingly aware of her own physical hungers that had been denied for over a year, ever since the accident . . . ever since Dave's death. She watched as a slow smile spread across his features, making his face seem less cruel. His hand came forward, and he touched a strand of her dark hair between this thumb and index finger.

"It must be fortune smiling on me. I'm glad you got lost."

Cait fought to shrug off the strong effect he had on her. My God, she was twenty-nine, hardly new to the world of men. Why was she acting dumbstruck, her tongue frozen in her throat and a peculiar aching beginning deep within her? Sudden anger aroused her and she took one step back, jutting her chin out and glaring up at him.

"On the contrary, señor, I am hardly lost! I'm supposed to meet a pilot from the Miron Corporation who will fly me directly to the Rio Colorado construction site."

Disbelief flared briefly in those leonine eyes that suddenly became hooded by thick ebony lashes. "You're C. F. Monahan?" he asked blackly.

"Yes, I am. Cait Monahan, from Brentworth. Are you the pilot?"

For a moment, Cait wasn't sure whether he was going to curse outright or stalk off. He stood there, hands resting tensely on his hips as he continued to stare down at her. An invisible current of tension grew between them, and Cait gripped her bag tightly, making her knuckles turn white.

"You must be Señor Tobbar," she finally managed.

His black hair dipped across his head as he bowed mockingly. He pushed the rebellious strands back, and one corner of his mouth twisted upward in a cool smile. "I see my reputation has already reached you, Señora Monahan."

She didn't bother to extend her hand, too shaken by his blatant advances. If he was embarrassed, he did not show it. After interminable seconds, he added in an almost purring tone, "I've been called many things at the construction site, but you can start out with Dominic if you prefer."

Mystified by his manner and dizzied by the almost physical caress of his voice, Cait murmured, "Obviously you weren't expecting a woman."

Dominic shook his head, his eyes stormy. "Obviously I wasn't. I hope you didn't bring a caravan of suitcases with you, because I'm in a hurry, and there isn't time to sit around here passing pleasantries."

Cait throttled her anger, setting her lips in a firm line. "Customs has already passed my two suitcases," she answered stiffly.

"Good. At least you travel light," he drawled lazily, and then turned to the man at the desk. Cait stood anchored to the spot, calmly watching him, amazed by his flagrant lack of respect for her. After all, as project superintendent for the behind-schedule project, she was his new boss. But she decided to say nothing. Once they got to the site and she picked up the reins of authority, she would deal with Dominic Tobbar's attitude. Now was not the time or place. She was tired from the long flight to Argentina, and he looked as if he had already put in a long, hard day. Tempers always flared when schedules weren't being met.

Dominic turned back to her. "Pablo will escort you to the plane." He indicated a dark-haired man approaching. "I'll be back in five minutes."

Cait had the childish urge to time him, but she didn't. Pablo smiled shyly, greeting her in broken English.

The plane, a twin-engine Beechcraft with the Miron insignia, stood on the apron, looking sleek and powerful. Cait climbed into the copilot's seat and strapped in, waiting for Dominic Tobbar to return. The clear night sky held thousands of blinking stars. She shivered. It was cooler than she had expected.

Dominic appeared exactly five minutes later. The light from the building slanted across his head and broad shoulders, reminding Cait of a knight who had just walked out of the dark ages. There was not an iota of wasted motion about him, and she felt herself being pulled into a vortex of capability that seemed to emanate from him. In a flash it struck her that, if he chose to, he could be a formidable adversary.

Sighing heavily, Cait faced forward. Once they were aloft, the lights of Buenos Aires quickly disappeared, to be replaced with velvet blackness. Unlike night flights over the States, where dots of lights always indicated small towns, Argentina remained closed, swathed in an ebony coat. Dominic trimmed up the aircraft, and Cait glanced over at him.

"How long will it take us to get to the site?"

His face had taken on an eerie green cast as the lighted instrument panel reflected off his features. "ETA is in two hours and ten minutes," he replied in a distant tone.

Cait mentally cursed him. Why was he being so damn hostile and abrupt? She tried once more. "It looks like you've put in a few hours today."

He tilted his head to appraise her slowly, as if deciding whether he should snap, snarl or bark. Cait's stomach knotted and her breath snagged. Then, as quickly as his savage expression had appeared, it was replaced by an unreadable mask. "Yes, it's been one hell of a day, and by the looks of it, there are going to be many more."

"I take it you weren't supposed to be the pilot for this trip?"

"No, I was not. I'm too damn busy to be playing chauffeur."

Cait tried to shrug off the tension building between them again. The atmosphere in the cabin was one kilowatt away from exploding. Compressing her lips, she frowned, trying to put all his abrupt, accusing statements together. "Didn't Señor Campos inform you of who I was?"

His mouth slit into an ugly smile. "If you mean, did he tell me the boss was going to be a woman, no. But then," he added darkly, readjusting the trim tab slightly, "Campos enjoys putting me on the defensive. So I guess I shouldn't be surprised at all."

She fell silent once again, reminding herself not to grip her hands so tightly in reaction. Concentrating on the throbbing of the engines, she finally began to relax and closed her eyes.

"How's Hank doing?"

Cait blinked her eyes in confusion. "What?"

He gave her a bored look, then returned his attention to the gauges. "I asked if Hank is going to make it."

She rubbed her eyes tiredly. "Last I heard, he had made it through surgery and was in the recovery room. The operation was a complete success."

She recalled her conversation with her boss, Chuck Goodell, who had sent her to Argentina after only two weeks of rest. She was sorry Hank Parker, former head of the pipeline project, had suffered a major heart attack, but she was relieved to be out in the field once more, away from the haunting memories of her dead husband.

Dominic nodded. "Good."

She slid back into the seat, wrapping her arms around her body to stay warm. Completely confused by Dominic Tobbar, she decided to try and sleep. Soon darkness calmed her and she dozed.

Her slumber was punctuated with bits and pieces of an old dream. She was cold, so very cold as she stood on the wrecked gas platform two miles off the Indonesian coast. She felt a snake of terror uncoiling within her as she watched the frenzied efforts of the rescue crew. It was one hundred and ten degrees and one hundred percent humidity, but she was cold to the bone, because Dave was trapped beneath the bent and twisted drilling tower, along with five other drillers. Sweat was running off her, and she felt the icy fingers of death around her heart...

Someone was calling, a voice from very far away, but it wasn't Dave's voice. Cait moaned, moving around in the seat. Suddenly she snapped awake, her eyes unseeing as the last fragments of the nightmare lingered.

"I asked if you were all right," Dominic Tobbar demanded.

Cait looked down to find a jacket tucked around her. She met his intense gaze. "No...I mean..." She licked her dry lips and pushed a strand of hair off her face. "I'm fine," she answered, her voice oddly husky.

"I thought you had malaria, or something, the way you suddenly broke out in a sweat. Did you just get back from the Orient?"

Cait was unable to answer his hard, staccato questions so soon after awakening from the grip of her nightmare. For an instant, she saw concern flicker in his gaze. It made his face look pleasant, almost boyish.

"Yes—Indonesia," she stumbled. She was perspiring heavily. Reaching for her canvas purse, she

pulled out a linen handkerchief and dabbed her forehead and cheeks. He didn't seem satisfied with her
answer. His gaze lingered hungrily on her features,
and she felt stripped and helpless beneath his probing
stare.

"We get a lot of malaria up in northern Argentina.
You looked like a classic case. Came on fast and
sudden. I have a thermos of coffee in the glove com-
partment," he added. "We both need some."

She was thankful for the diversion and relieved by
his less-aggressive stance. After pouring the hot liquid
into two plastic cups, Cait sat back and sipped it
silently. She was still trembling. God, why wouldn't
the dreams go away? Why did she have to relive the
horrible accident again and again? She swallowed
hard, trying to shore up her battered emotions. The
coffee was warm and comforting in her hands, and
it began to soothe her jangled nerves.

"Better?" Dominic inquired.

She nodded, managing a weak smile. "Yes, thank
you."

"What did they do, haul you off one project and
throw this one in your lap?"

"Almost," she admitted, glad that he was being
more civil. "I finished off an oil platform near Java
two and a half weeks ago."

He smiled thinly, banking the plane toward an un-
seen area far below. "Well, you're either very good
at what you do or you're the only one Brentworth
could find to send down to this mess."

She was still too shaken to think of an adequate
defense. As usual, she would have to prove her abil-
ities all over again. If she had been a man, the chal-

lenge would never been thrown.

The plane came back on an even keel beneath his touch, and he looked over at her, studying her left hand where she still wore the plain gold wedding band Dave had given her nearly five years ago. "Your husband going to be joining you at the site?" he asked acidly.

Rebuffed, Cait found it nearly impossible to hide the hurt of freshly healed wounds. A lump formed in her throat, and she swallowed hard. "No...he...he's dead. He died a year ago, in a platform accident."

Dominic sat back, pursing his lips, glancing at her out of the corner of his eye. "I'm sorry," he muttered.

Cait wasn't sure he was apologizing for asking the question so nastily or for Dave's death. It took every bit of will power to control the anguish that threatened to explode within her. She sighed softly. Why was Dominic Tobbar able to shred her carefully built walls in moments, when no one else had done so in almost a year?

"Then you're a women's libber...a feminist?" he prodded, his tone less cruel but nonetheless probing.

Cait detected a glimmer of humor in his tone, and she smiled, closing her eyes and relaxing. "The only label you have to remember, Señor Tobbar, is that I'm project superintendent. Don't let the rest concern you."

She did not look to see the effect her words had on him, but she heard him laugh softly, a rich, deep sound that filled the cabin.

"Campos is in for a big surprise, I'm afraid," he murmured, and then fell silent.

Minutes later, he guided the Beechcraft onto a

rough dirt airstrip feebly lit on either side. It looked dangerous, and Cait made a mental note to make sure it was properly lighted in the future. The plane rolled up to a waiting sedan and jeep. Switching off the engine, Dominic turned to her.

"Welcome to Rio Colorado, Señora Monahan." He smiled coldly and opened the door. "You'll be in the very capable hands of Señor Campos from now on."

Cait pulled the jacket from around her shoulders and handed it to him. "Thanks for the loan."

He nodded, and an inquiring glint shone in his eyes. Silence hung between them, and Cait's breath caught in her throat as she fell under his disturbing gaze. Then his features relaxed and the impenetrable wall around him seemed to melt away. His mouth, pliable and strong, mesmerized her. He smiled slowly, and reached out toward her.

Cait swayed forward in response, feeling tenderness and concern flowing from him, charged with an almost animalistic desire . . . for her. A shiver of longing made her tremble as if he had actually run his hand up her arm and placed his mouth lightly on hers.

But, still without touching her, he allowed his hand to drop back to his long, muscular thigh. "Too bad you weren't lost," he murmured, and then he disappeared into the night. Cait felt as if something of great value had slipped from her grasp.

Chapter Two

THE GLARE OF HEADLIGHTS blinded Cait as she stepped carefully from the plane to the ground. A soft layer of dust beneath her feet told her it was going to be a dirty, grimy job.

"Señora Monahan! Welcome, welcome. I am Jorge Campos, site superintendent for the Miron Corporation." The voice came from a dark human shape approaching from the direction of the headlights. Señor Campos emerged from the shadows and pressed a wet kiss to her hand. She withdrew it quickly and smiled weakly.

"Thank you, Señor Campos."

"Please, come right this way. Pedro will get your bags. Step into my car and we'll be underway. I'm sure you're very tired from your long trip. I trust it was a pleasant flight?"

Campos's rounded features struck Cait as almost moon-like. His heavy, droopy eyelids made him look as if he were asleep. He was half a head shorter than Cait and looked ill at ease. "The flight was fine," she said, sliding into the sedan and straining to see beyond the lights, to the project. The third shift was working, and under the harsh glare of portable light units, she could detect bulldozers and cranes working in a cacophony of sound. The project must be near the river, she thought, suddenly anxious to explore her new territory.

Campos leaped in on the passenger's side and rapidly gave orders in Spanish to Pedro, who stowed the bags in the trunk and took the driver's seat. They sped down the dirt runway.

"We have been anxiously awaiting your arrival, Señora Monahan," Campos continued. "When Señor Goodell informed us you were a woman, we were even more pleased."

I'll bet, Cait thought, gripping the seat and using her left arm as a cushion against the bumping, swaying vehicle. "I'm sure it was a surprise," she answered drily.

"But he never said it would be a beautiful woman! This is double luck for us."

Now Cait knew he was being deceptive, and fixed a tight smile on her lips. At least she could rely on Dominic to be truthful—if blunt. She sighed. Maybe Campos was just nervous.

"You Argentinians are very complimentary," she said in way of thanks.

"Camp Two barracks is only six kilometers away, señora. Pedro has gone to a great deal of trouble to make sure your quarters are clean, but unfortunately Patagonia is a dusty place. You will have a two-room cottage that is situated near the rest of the supervisory-personnel barracks."

"Don't apologize for the dirt, Señor Campos. I'm used to living in harsh conditions, as I'm sure you are."

Maybe she was overly tired, but she had a sudden desire to laugh outright at Campos's use of the word "cottage." It was sure to be a prefab modular structure covered with metal sheeting. She could picture it now—hastily assembled housing put together by a subcontractor, with a metal folding bed and single light fixture suspended from the ceiling. Electricity was hard to come by in Argentina, and at most construction sites it was supplied by diesel generators.

"I'm grateful to you for sending Señor Tobbar to get me," Cait commented. "I understand he was pulled away from his work."

Campos shrugged eloquently. Compared to well-muscled Dominic Tobbar, he looked skinny. "I was planning on coming, but unfortunately I was tied up in a meeting with the site procurement manager." He smiled. "Pay no attention to Tobbar, señora. He is constantly griping about anything that he does not want to do." Campos waved his hand in emphasis.

"I see," she murmured. So maybe her first impression of Dominic Tobbar had been right—a misfit who didn't get along with management even though he was part of the supervisory team who ran this project. She tucked Campos's reaction away along with her own evaluation. Sooner or later, Dominic's true nature would become clear to her. If he was a troublemaker, she'd get rid of him, or anyone else who might be slowing the project down.

The sedan pulled to a halt in front of a small modular structure, and Pedro leaped out. "It isn't much, señora," he said, opening the door for her with an apologetic smile. "Please, make yourself comfortable."

To Cait's delight, a floor lamp had been installed in one corner. It burned feebly when Pedro flipped the switch, and seemed to soften the glare from the ceiling fixture. The plywood walls were barren, and a cot stood in the far corner, with several green blankets folded neatly at the foot. Pedro set her bags down carefully, grinning broadly, his crooked teeth white against his reddish skin. He took off his hard hat and bowed.

"It eez bueno to have you, señora," he said.

Cait smiled warmly and touched his shoulder. *"Muchas gracias,* Pedro," she murmured. The Spanish rolled off her tongue in a stilted and unfamiliar manner. She would have to bone up on it in a hurry if she wanted to communicate effectively with everyone.

Pedro's weathered features lit with pleasure. Bowing again, he scurried out. Campos laughed. "I've scheduled a meeting at 11:00 A.M. tomorrow. I'm sure you want to catch up on your sleep before starting."

Cait dropped her purse on the cot. "On the contrary, Señor Campos, I want to see you at my office at 8:00 A.M. sharp, and I expect a general meeting of all supervisory personnel to be called for 8:30. I don't want anyone missing or tardy, is that understood?"

Campos's smile vanished. His black eyes became hooded as he stared up at her. "You realize it is 2:09 A.M. right now?" he said.

She nodded. "Quite aware of it. Have a driver pick me up at 6:00, will you? Good night."

Cait awoke with a start. Her watch read five-thirty. The chill in the shack was a stark contrast to the wet humidity of Indonesia. Fumbling for her jeans, she slipped them on and reached for a long-sleeved khaki shirt, then stepped outside into the clear morning air.

She was facing east, where the orange sky was growing brighter by the minute. Soon the sun would lift its fiery edge above the gray hills.

Her ears picked up the sounds of working bull-dozers and cranes, and she walked around the corner, searching for the source of the welcome noise. Her gaze focused on a distant green strip of land which surrounded the Rio Colorado. Harsh scars were evident where the earth had been removed to make an access road paralleling the pipeline. Somewhere beyond the pipe-laying operation was the bridge-working area. As soon as the meeting was over, she would check its progress.

The thought of the bridge brought back an immediate and physical sensation of Dominic Tobbar. Turning, Cait wondered if he had gotten some sleep or if he had gone back to work on the bridge. She made a wry face, and went inside. Why did Dominic seem to stay on her mind?

Brushing her hair back, she fixed it into a chignon at the nape of her slender neck. She dug into her cosmetic bag, and put some lip protector on her mouth, wanting to discourage the imminent chapping that always took place in a desert environment. Holding up a small mirror, she was pleased with the way she looked. Her eyes were wide and alert, filled with excitement.

Pedro arrived at exactly six. He raced around the vehicle and opened the door with a flourish. Cait thanked him and slid in. There was a white Brentworth hard hat on the seat, with the words "Project Superintendent Monahan" on it. Pedro climbed in and motioned for her to take it.

"Eez for you, señora. I make it. You like?"

Cait set the hard hat on her head. It fit perfectly, and she felt very much at home wearing it. "I like very much, Pedro. Let's go to the office now, shall we?"

"*Bueno. Sí, sí.*"

The six-kilometer drive was brutal. A column of dust rose fifteen feet in the air behind the pickup truck as Pedro sped toward their destination. They wove in and out of the construction buildings until they finally arrived at a complex of six office trailers. Cait thanked Pedro and climbed up a set of rickety wooden stairs into the mobile office.

Taking off the hard hat, Cait set it on her desk and ran a finger across the top. A streak of fine dust coated her hand, and she wiped it off on her jeans. All the windows were opened and screened, indicating the air-conditioning unit was not working. She grinned, leaned against the desk and folded her arms across her chest.

By the time Campos arrived, she was ensconced behind her desk, reading through reports from each of the site supervisors.

"Señora Monahan—I didn't realize you'd be here

so early," he began, taking off his hard hat.

She smiled perfunctorily, noticing that he wore starched, pressed khakis. He looked quite dapper and tailored, and she was pleased that he took trouble with his appearance. "I get up with the birds," she told him. "There's hot coffee over there, if you want some."

Campos looked at the pot and touched his thin black mustache. "Uh...no, thank you, señora. We Argentinians drink *maté* instead of coffee." He offered a weak smile of apology, went to the cupboard below the pot and drew out a heating element and some loose green tea.

"Your national drink?" she inquired.

"Very much so. You must try it soon." He tinkered nervously with the tea, dropped the plastic spoon twice and glanced up.

"This is a, uh...rare privilege to work with a woman, señora. I...I mean, we have never had the opportunity..."

She set the report down. "Please, Señor Campos, relax. This is a new experience for me too. I've never worked in South America. My Spanish is extremely rusty, and I don't know any Italian or French. So who is at a worse disadvantage here?"

Campos gave a slight shrug and drew a wooden chair opposite her desk. "Do you always have the right words to say, señora? Even the savage jaguar would purr beneath your diplomacy." He smiled broadly and lifted his cup in a toast.

Cait nodded, pursing her lips. The only jaguar she knew was a tall, dark-haired civil engineer who didn't cool down under any number of diplomatic strokes.

She was curious as to what did contain Dominic Tobbar. He was a willful warrior out to fight his own personal wars, it would seem. She forced him from her mind, concentrating instead on Campos, who had been sipping his tea cautiously.

"Tell me, Señor Campos—"

"Por favor, call me Jorge," he insisted.

"Very well, Jorge, give me your opinion of why this project is so far behind schedule."

His black brows drew downward in thought. "I mean no insult, Señora Monahan, but Hank—Señor Parker—was a very sick man for a long time. He was ailing for three months before he had his heart attack, and toward the end, he was putting in short, six-hour days."

Cait nodded. "Instead of the usual twelve to sixteen," she returned grimly.

"Sí. Our business is not measured in hours, but days and contracts. Anyway, one month before the attack, he was in perhaps two or three hours daily and trying to run it from his quarters. It just didn't work."

She toyed absently with a pencil, keeping her eyes fixed on him. "Why didn't you alert Brentworth of the problem?"

"Hank was in charge. I could only express my view, as I am still bound to follow his orders. My company is supplying men and materials. Project management is supplied by Brentworth."

Cait sat back, rocking thoughtfully in her chair. A good supervisor, no matter what company he worked for, would have done something much sooner. Perhaps Campos was as ineffective as he looked. She frowned. Still, a man—or a woman—didn't get to be site supervisor by lying on his backside, getting a suntan. She sat back down with a thump.

"There has to be something else, Jorge..."

The Argentine set the cup down heavily and nodded. "Sí, there is. Not a something but a someone, señora."

Cait cocked her head to one side, listening intently. "Oh? A Brentworth official?"

"No. Unfortunately, one of our people. Dominic Tobbar."

"Go on," she coaxed, all her senses alert.

Campos rose, rubbing his mustache in an irritated manner. "He is amoral, señora. He works only for his part of the project and cares nothing for the rest of the schedule. His work gangs are continually fighting with other groups of men at the bridge work. There are Miron's rules and then there are Tobbar's rules. I've been completely stifled by the agitation he has caused between the labor unions. He treats his work gangs differently than the other laborers are treated, and then a furor arises. At least once every day I get called down there to mediate between the bickering sides." Campos chewed on his thin lower lip, his expression mirroring his frustration.

Cait strode over to the personnel cabinet and went through it until she found a file marked Tobbar. She scanned the brief information. "He has impeccable records, Jorge." She flipped through to another series. "Recommendations from other projects via Miron officials." Frowning, she dug deeper, trying to read the Spanish. "Am I wrong, or are there reprimands in here that I'm not seeing?"

"No, señora, no reprimands...until now."

She closed the file. "Why now?"

Campos turned, studying her. "I'm sure you've seen it before, señora. A bright young engineer becomes the darling of a company and is spoiled by a string of successes. When he finally gets a project that is far beyond his experience and capability, he blames everyone else for a failing schedule."

"Yes, I've seen them come and go," she agreed. But somehow Dominic Tobbar did not strike her in that light. He was abrupt and arrogant but not, she felt, sloppy or ineffective. Why would he be working long hours if he didn't care? "Anything else?" she prodded Campos stubbornly.

The Argentine supervisor frowned also. "What you can't possibly know is that the Tobbar name in Argentina is one of the oldest and most highly respected. Dominic is the only son and has been given everything. He is in a very embarrassing situation presently, because of the scheduling. He helped cause it, by flaunting union rules, and work stoppages have been the result. At this point, he would willingly throw the blame elsewhere, because of his stature in society, señora. One who comes from such an old family must keep up appearances."

"I see," Cait murmured, tapping her fingers on top of the file, deep in thought. "A spoiled rich boy who can't take it when the going gets tough?"

"Precisely!" Campos began to pace, placing his hands behind his back. "I tell you, Señora Monahan, you'd best get rid of him. Quickly. I was going to present all the evidence to Hank, but when he became sick, I withheld, it because I didn't want to put any more pressure on him."

Cait looked at her watch. "We've got five minutes,

Jorge. Let's get over to the conference trailer."

The sun was rising rapidly now, and Cait felt the wind beginning to pick up. She shaded her eyes, enjoying the rich greenness of the Rio Colorado. It was eight-thirty when they arrived at the larger trailer. Cait was met by fifteen inquiring men. The general level of noise died down to near silence as she stepped up to the long rows of tables and chairs. Doffing her hard hat, she nodded. *"Buenos días,* gentlemen. Please, sit down and make yourselves comfortable." Cait moved toward the other end of the conference table. The construction men stole quick glances at her, and she returned their curious gazes with a solemn look. Lifting her chin, she asked Jorge, "Señor, is everyone present and accounted for?"

"No, Señor Tobbar is missing," he said, his voice heavy with checked anger.

"Very well. Let's get started, then. In the meantime, have someone get Señor Tobbar up here now."

Campos's expression was one of caged delight. He picked up a radio to page the tardy civil engineer. Cait quickly launched into what she expected of her group. Weekly reports must be on her desk by two o'clock Friday afternoon, and she gave explicit instructions on what she expected. If the men had anticipated a woman who would softly ask them to supply the information, they were mistaken. Each man, his face wind- and weather-sculpted, sat at rapt attention as she ticked off the requirements in successive order. Her voice and manner were firm, without being pushy. She noted that most of the men had drawn out small note-pads and were making hasty marks. That was a good sign.

The door was suddenly jerked open, and Cait halted

in mid-sentence, her pulse leaping wildly as Dominic Tobbar strode into the office, red mud splattered over his jeans and boots.

His gaze raked the assemblage, resting finally on Cait. Her stomach tightened in reaction, and her skin flushed infuriatingly as their eyes locked. She squeezed the pen in her hand until her fingertips whitened. For the first time since Dave's death, she felt unsure of herself on the job.

Dominic was treating her like an adversary, an enemy. Didn't his unexplained advances of last night mean anything? Why was he purposely trying to embarrass her?

Her heart pounding, Cait motioned toward the only vacant chair in the room. Her voice was high when she said, "Thank you for coming, Señor Tobbar. If you can spare a few minutes, I'll make this as brief as possible so you can return to work."

Dominic's eyes narrowed as if to study her in minute detail. She felt weak under his stripping gaze but managed to maintain her composure. Campos spoke before she could. "Señora Monahan has a great deal more patience with your impertinence than I do, Tobbar. You are late, and there is no excuse for it."

Cait felt the entire room stiffen with tension. Dominic turned slowly, gauging Campos from across the table. "Well, maybe if you could begin supplying some spare parts for my cranes, there wouldn't be unexpected breakdowns, Señor Campos. I ordered new sheaves six months ago, and where are they? I was just out there repairing the boom-point sheave that's bound the cable up for the third time this week."

"Your cranes! Your men! When are you going to

learn to become part of the team effort?" Campos
snarled.

"There is no team effort, Campos! There's only
you, Cirre and your little clique." Dominic glared
down the table at Cait. "And now we've got a woman
sitting in Hank's place, and this site is going to go
to hell for sure."

Cait was suddenly furious. "Señor Tobbar, I don't
give a damn what you think about women. Keep your
personal observations out of this meeting." Her voice
quavered as he swung around, his gaze momentarily
stunning her. "If you have any personal opinions to
express, do so to me in private. And Señor Campos,
I suggest the same of you. Both of you sit down and
shut up until this meeting is over. If you want to
discuss these allegations further, we will do so in my
office and not waste the precious time of the other
supervisors, who are trying very hard to get back on
schedule. Is that understood?"

A pulse pounded in her throat as she stared down
the table at them. Red-faced, Campos sat down and
Cait turned her gaze to Dominic. She thought she saw
that same veiled humor in his fiercely glinting eyes,
but, bowing in her direction, he too pulled a chair up
and sat down.

A collective sigh of relief rose from the men as she
began to speak to each supervisor in charge of various
sections of the project. Each time Cait's gaze swept
around the room, she was aware of Dominic's un-
wavering stare. His curiosity only irritated her more.
Was he deliberately trying to be bothersome? She
fearlessly met his eyes when it was his turn to report
on the bridge status. Her throat ached with the un-

spoken tension between them.

He wiped his long fingers on his thigh. "Considering the time lost due to broken equipment, my men are making good progress in building the cofferdams. The PZ-38 sheet piling is in place, the area has been pumped dry and the excavation completed."

Cait nodded, scribbling down a few notes. "What is the status of the reinforcing steel for the pier base slab?" she asked.

"We began placing the rebar today. If"—he glanced significantly at Campos and then at the nervous project procurement supervisor, Cirre—"I don't experience any more needless breakdowns of equipment, we'll begin pouring concrete in two days. Providing the weather holds."

She caught the underlying growl in his voice and stole a look at Cirre. The Spaniard colored deeply but said nothing. Campos's lips compressed into a thin, menacing line. Dominic was almost smiling. What was going on among these three men?

"If there is nothing more, Señor Tobbar," she said, managing to hold his amber gaze despite her tingling awareness of him, "you may return to the river."

Dominic rose in one fluid motion. "If there is," he said, "you'll hear from me."

Her heart was pumping strongly, and her pulse leaped again at the challenge in his voice. She fixed an icy smile on her face. "I'm sure I will."

The rest of the meeting went smoothly. When it came to question Benito Cirre, the project procurement supervisor, who was in charge of purchasing the materials, equipment and subcontract services necessary for each area of the project, he appeared nervous.

"Señora," he replied in poor English, "everything is fine, fine in my department. You have no need to worry. All is well."

"Do you have a scheduler, Señor Cirre?" she demanded, stung by his implied suggestion that his department need not be investigated.

"Of course not! I have served as the chief purchasing agent on ten other projects for the Miron Corporation, and never once has my decision been questioned..." His voice trailed off as he saw the anger in her eyes.

"I'm not questioning your wisdom, Señor Cirre," Cait remarked coldly. "Despite your experience, I have had a scheduler on every project I've been on." She wrote the name "Louie Henning" on her pad.

Cirre's coffee-brown face turned deep plum, and he struggled to retort. But Campos placed a warning hand on his arm, and Cirre released a long, exasperated breath of air and sank further down into his chair, glaring at the table.

Much relieved to have avoided an even more heated confrontation, Cait reminded the rest of the men that she would be speaking to them individually on the site over the next few days. With a weary sigh, she adjourned the meeting.

Chapter Three

IT WAS LATE AFTERNOON by the time Cait was able to pull free of her office and get Pedro to drive her down to the bridge-construction area. She had rolled up her long-sleeved shirt in an effort to cool off. To her disgust, Patagonian dust gathered on every paper and object. The windows had to remain open, and the screens did nothing but invite the reddish-yellowish film indoors.

Picking up her white hard hat, she threw it on her head and left word with her Italian secretary, Filipo, as to where she would be. Filipo was sulking after having been told in no uncertain terms that he and all other office personnel would have to be at work at eight, not nine, from now on. Banker's hours were for those who could afford them.

As she descended down the wooden dusty steps, Cait was sure everyone was silently cursing her. Schedules were a bitch to make, and superintendents were thoroughly disliked for enforcing them. But then, Cait reasoned, climbing into the battered white pickup, she didn't get paid to be nice.

The silence was a friend, in comparison to the ringing of the telephone, the constant influx of people to her office and the squawk of radios as the different supervisory personnel paged one another or sent instructions over the crowded airways.

Contentment stole over Cait as she observed the activity at the bridge-crossing site. A crane with one hundred and eighty feet of boom was sitting solidly on a barge anchored in the Rio Colorado. She watched the graceful arc as it swung its main lifthook block from the cofferdam to the shore to pick up another load of form work. Somewhere in her wandering thoughts, Cait was aware of being glad Dominic had gotten his barge crane back into operation.

She studied the greenness of the lush growth bordering both sides of the lazily moving Rio Colorado. The water was a dirty jade color, and sunlight danced off its surface. Pedro slowed the truck as they entered the bridge-crossing supply and materials buildings area—shacks of galvanized steel coated with a permanent layer of yellow dust.

Cait's brows drew downward as she spotted at least ten laborers languishing in the shade. "What are they doing?" she asked Pedro as he braked the truck to a halt.

Her driver shrugged eloquently. Cait's anger soared. Leaving the truck, she walked toward the men.

"What's going on here?" she demanded, stopping in front of them. She recognized by the gray color on their hard hats that they were ironworkers, not laborers. The gang boss, a hulking man stripped to the waist, stood up, glaring at her.

"Who the hell are you?" he retorted in a thick German accent.

"That's my question, mister," she snapped back. "Are you in charge of this crew?"

The German's meaty red face became set. He squinted his blue eyes, reading the title that Pedro had painted on her hard hat. His expression slowly changed, and he resumed chewing a huge wad of tobacco lodged in his protruding right cheek.

"I'm in charge," he rumbled.

"Your name?"

"Dolph."

"Why are you standing around, Dolph? It's past siesta and well past union coffee break."

"Boss told us to take it easy for a while. We're just trying to stay outa the sun."

It was hot. She was thirsty, and her throat was tight with tension. "Who's your boss, Dolph?"

"Herr Tobbar."

Her eyes lowered and she retreated a step, pushing the hard hat back and rubbing her forehead. "All right, where can I find him? Or is he on a break too?"

"*Nein.* He's down by the blueprint shack."

She gritted her teeth and turned away, walking quickly between the buildings. She had gone no more than two hundred feet when she spotted him coming out of a print shack, with a roll of blueprints under his arm. "Señor Tobbar!" she yelled.

As he turned and looked in her direction, Cait saw that his face was lined with fatigue. An unreadable mask settled over his features as she approached, her heart pounding in her dry throat. He waited for her, one hand resting lazily against his hip as she halted a foot from him.

"Is that shack empty?" she demanded coldly, pointing to the one he had just left.

His expression lightened. "Yes."

"Good. Come inside. There's something you and I need to discuss immediately."

His expression remained curious as he obeyed. Cait turned on her heel, her green eyes glinting with barely contained anger. He appeared to barely notice as he set the prints down on a table.

"What's on your mind, señora?" he asked softly, his gaze moving recklessly over her body.

Cait shivered. Her anger evaporated under his inspection, and to her dismay, she felt her body tremble into awareness. Doggedly she said, "I just ran into one of your ironworker gangs. Dolph and his men are sitting around as if they don't have a thing in the world to do." She swallowed, her throat scratchy and her heart pulsing erratically as he raised his yellow eyes to her face. "I find it hard to believe they have been instructed to take it easy, when we're so far behind schedule. Are they still on siesta or is this an unscheduled coffee break?"

Dominic folded his arms across his chest. "Neither," he snapped.

Cait removed her hard hat, wiping her brow with the back of her arm. "Unless you have a good excuse, I—"

His nostrils flared and his arms tightened. "Señora Monahan," he whispered throatily, "I can't use them this instant, owing to the crane failure this morning. I can't send them home, because I'm going to need them in another hour. They're ironworkers and they won't do laborers' work, because of union laws. What do you suggest I do with them? Hang them on sky hooks?"

Her fingers dug into the hat in reaction to the ve-
hemence in his voice. Her palms were wet with perspiration, and she fought back from mouthing a curse.
"I don't care what you do with them, as long as they
aren't standing around! Why do you think this project
is behind? It couldn't be because your men are standing around, could it?"

His eyes glowed with a terrible darkness, and Cait
shuddered as he stepped toward her in one swift motion. He was so close, she could smell the raw animal
scent of his body, and she felt dizzy.

His hand shot out, closing around her upper arm,
drawing her harshly against his hard, unyielding chest.
Cait inhaled a sharp breath and tried to push away.
It was impossible. It was as if his wind- and sun-
hardened flesh had been fashioned out of tempered
steel. Her senses reeled.

"I see they've got to you already," he whispered
hoarsely, the quiver in his voice making her wince.
"Start your investigation back among the paper push-
ers in the office!" His lips curled as he moved an inch
closer. "If you really care about the truth, search there!
Don't come out here and get on my back about a few
workers standing around for an hour or two. It's my
job to get a bridge built with second-hand equipment,
lousy-fitting spare parts and back orders that are six
months old. What the hell are you doing? It's your
job to make sure I get the things I need, so my men
don't have to stand around!"

He jerked away so suddenly that Cait had to catch
herself. He strode away, jerked up the blueprint roll
and slammed the door behind him.

She trembled, closing her eyes and fighting back

tears of rage. Campos was right. Dominic Tobbar was nothing but a troublemaker who was always ready to foist the problems back on upper management. Grabbing her hat from the table, she walked stiffly out of the shack.

Cait lost track of time as she continued to cross check records of when materials had been bid, purchase orders issued, equipment finally delivered and spare parts reordered. By the time she looked up to get a cup of coffee, night had thrown its black cape across the desert. Pushing a thick strand of hair from her temple, she threw another pile of purchase orders on the table. Her stomach growled, but she ignored it. The clash with Dominic had destroyed her appetite completely.

It was nearly eleven-thirty when she laid her head down on the stack of pink-and-white documents to doze for a few minutes. A noise, a door opening, made her jerk up. She looked toward the entrance, her eyes large and dazed with tiredness. It took two full seconds to realize she had given a small cry of alarm. Dominic Tobbar stood in the doorway, filling it with his bulk, the light behind him making him look like a nightmarish shadow.

"I didn't mean to startle you."

Cait rubbed her eyes, fighting off grogginess. His field boots sounded hollowly in the trailer as he walked over to the table. She looked up at him guardedly, feeling vulnerable from waking, without the facade of her supervisory functions to mask her mobile features. He set a green bottle down and placed two white styrofoam cups in front of her. Grasping a chair, he sat down opposite her, his arms draped casually on the table.

The silence deepened. Cait felt an almost tangible friction beginning to build between them. "Look," she began, her voice husky, "I'm—"

"I owe you an apology," he interrupted softly, his mouth quirking at one corner. "I deserve your anger. I shouldn't have lost my temper out there this afternoon. It isn't your fault this site is a mess." He gestured toward the bottle. "Wine from Mendoza. Best burgundy in the country. A peace offering after today's events." His eyes were hooded as he continued to stare at her. "I'd like to apologize for being so forward, if it offended you."

She stared at him, not quite able to cope with his change in attitude. This could not be the Dominic Tobbar she knew. No, this man was speaking in an even, conciliatory tone, his face mirroring the sincerity of his words. And his voice—Cait shivered. It was as if a cat were caressing her flesh with its rough tongue. Gone was the stonelike rage from the sculptured planes of his face. Instead his eyes were warm and—did she see hesitancy? Why? It certainly wasn't fear. Dominic was afraid of nothing and no one.

The sound of the cork popping and the gurgle of wine hitting the bottom of the cups drew her back to the present. He offered her a drink.

"Truce?"

Cait took the cup. Their fingers touched, and a jolt of electric shock flowed up her arm. She froze for only a second, caught off guard by the coaxing tone in his voice. Taking a quick swallow, she nodded.

"Fair enough," she agreed, her voice suddenly weak.

The friction that had bound them disappeared like fog struck by the sun. The wine was sweet and delicious, and Cait felt its warmth spreading through her entire body. She fell back against the chair, her head tilted, her eyes meeting his golden gaze.

A smile edged his mouth. "You don't trust me, but then, I don't blame you."

She managed a sour grimace. "Some people just don't make good first impressions." How vividly she remembered her powerful reaction to his weathered features and the grace of his well-muscled body.

Dominic gauged her in silence, his fingers lightly smoothing the edge of the purchase orders. "Despite my reputation and the last twenty-four hours, you're still holding off on a final judgment?"

Her brows rose in curiosity, and she met his eyes fearlessly. "Frankly, Señor Tobbar, I don't know what to feel about you." She was lying. She knew very well what she was feeling, but she quelled the hollow ache deep inside and motioned toward a pile of documents. "Because you're right about supplies being delayed an inordinately long time. There's no excuse for it that I can find so far."

He drained his cup and leaned back in the chair. For the first time Cait saw the exhaustion in his face. It was evident in the slouch of his body and the lines furrowing his brow. So, she thought, he hid his tiredness just as much as she did. She was delighted. She was beginning to understand him.

"How many hours have you put in today?" she asked.

He snorted softly. "I should ask the same of you."

"It's my job," she retorted, keeping her voice even.

"Mine too."

Cait managed a sour grin, setting the half-empty cup back down on the desk and moving the stack of documents in front of them. "Well, you look as exhausted as I feel at this moment."

"On the contrary," he said softly, his voice a caress that made Cait tremble, "you look lovely."

She colored fiercely. "I look like hell and I feel like hell so let's let it go at that, shall we? In the meantime give me the benefit of your concern, and pick out which ones apply most seriously to the bridge-building effort."

Dominic straightened and dutifully began riffling through them. In a matter of minutes, he had sorted them. Cait closed her eyes for a moment, the letters blurring on the pink paper. Forcing herself to ignore the momentary cue that her body was ready to fold, she concentrated on each word.

"Your crane sheaves."

"Yes, six months late."

She put the papers down, rubbing her face. She could feel the grit of Patagonian dust on her skin and had a wild urge to hurry back to her quarters and wash her skin free of the grime.

Suddenly she found herself wanting to talk with him freely. Lifting her head, she found him watching her. She remembered the color of his eyes that afternoon when he had rounded on her in the print shack. They had turned a raw umber that reminded her of a black cloud laced with lightning. Gold meant that he was more relaxed and more cooperative. She would have to remember that small cue when dealing with him in the future.

"So what's the quickest way to get your sheaves?"

"Get them in Bahia Blanca, from one of the many drilling suppliers. Then have them priority-freighted out here."

She rose a trifle unsteadily, dizziness washing over her, which she automatically forced away. "Okay, make up a purchase requisition and have it on my desk first thing tomorrow morning."

If she had said the sky was falling in, she didn't think his reaction could be any more obvious. He rose, disbelief etched in the slackness of his square jaw. Again that unspoken tension began to swirl around her, and she pressed her lips together. "Well, what is it?" she demanded, angry.

"You're serious, aren't you?"

Cait sighed heavily. "Of course I am."

"Cirre is going to scream at the top of his skinny little lungs tomorrow when he finds out you've bypassed purchasing and bought materials outside his suppliers' list."

She made an irritated gesture. It was getting late, and she was becoming snappish and bitchy. "Señor Tobbar," she began as evenly as possible, "it's been a long day. We're both beat. I don't care, frankly, what Cirre is going to do. I do care what you do about this problem, and I expect my orders to be carried out quickly. Now, if you'll excuse me, I'm going to try and get a few hours' sleep."

He shook his head, a genuine smile on his face, then opened the trailer door for her. "Let me drive you over. I think Pedro already headed back to camp."

They rode along in silence. Cait, having learned years ago to catch naps whenever possible, curled up in a corner, using the hard hat to cushion her head as the truck jolted over the rutted road. Within seconds, she was spiraling into sleep.

Groggily she became aware of a gentle pressure on her shoulder shaking her back into wakefulness. Strong, pliant fingers slid along the thin fabric of her shirt with a gentle touch. It was a pleasant, almost forgotten sensation, and Cait turned her head, her eyes half-opened. Dominic's face showed concern as he leaned toward her, giving her another shake.

"When you sleep, you nose-dive," he muttered.

She managed a vulnerable smile, sitting up in the darkened cab. Her hard hat clunked down on her thigh and then hit the floorboards. As she leaned forward to retrieve it, the pins that had held her mahogany hair in a tight knot at the nape of her neck became loosened, spilling the cascade across her shoulders and down below her breasts.

"I learned a long time ago to grab a few minutes whenever I could," she was saying as she straightened back up. With the thick tresses soft around her face, and her eyes wide open, she suddenly felt much less an engineer and much more a woman.

Dominic's gaze was riveted on her upturned face. He leaned forward, his fingers slipping behind her neck, drawing her into a vortex of wild sensations. Her lips parted, ready . . . willing to feel the touch of his mouth on hers. He brushed her lips lightly, and a small moan of pleasure slid from her throat. His fingers tightened, became more demanding, pulling her closer. This time, his strong mouth smothered her lips in a hungry, searching kiss that kindled the banked fires of her body. Cait felt the heat building rapidly, and she fought against the heady urgency forcing her to succumb to his demands. His tongue invaded her mouth, searching the warmth of her, coaxing her own tongue to seek union with his...throwing her into a mindless spin of sensation...of hungry desire on the verge of ecstasy.

Suddenly he dragged his mouth from hers, his breath ragged, his eyes narrowed with golden fire. Cait could only stare, her bruised, parted lips throbbing. She saw confusion and desire in his burning gaze and was puzzled by his reaction. He moved his hand almost apologetically from her slender neck to her shoulder and finally took it away altogether. Cait looked away, feeling the inner ache of what he had coaxed into life. He had already known what she now realized—it was not the time or place, and that revelation hurt. She could barely think—only feel. There were memories of Dave's kisses...of the way he kissed and the way Dominic had forcefully awakened her desires. Cait slowly met his eyes, needing to see him...

He stroked her hair in a tender gesture. "You've had a long day. It's probably better you get some sleep..." His voice was unsteady, thick.

As she murmured good night and stepped from the truck, she wondered if she had imagined the imperceptible softening around his mouth and the hungry, veiled look in his eyes. She stumbled into her quarters. A part of her gloried in that fleeting, unshielded moment when Dominic had looked at her with pure physical desire.

Chapter Four

By LATE AFTERNOON the next day, Cait broke free of the paper work. Everyone was taking a two-hour siesta after lunch, so she decided to drive the company truck around the site in an effort to dispel the lingering frustration of having confronted Cirre earlier. Touring the northern perimeter, she eyed huge arsenals of supplies surrounded by six-foot-high cyclone fences. Stealing and pilferage weren't unusual. Much of it could be halted by a good guard service, but she hadn't been impressed with the guards she'd seen so far. As she drove up to a small annex gate, she met another truck coming out.

Dominic Tobbar flashed a dazzling smile of welcome as he left his truck and sauntered over. He looked more vital and alive than she had yet seen him. She returned the smile, her heartbeat increasing from unexpected joy, as she said, "You look happier than usual."

He put one foot on the running board and rested an arm against the window frame. "Ordering those crane sheaves has done it."

"I'm glad. You seem like a new person."

He grinned at her warmly. "Better than my angry self."

Cait agreed. Again she felt unbalanced by him. Dave had been so steady, so consistent. But Dominic was volatile, unpredictable. Her voice lost some of its brightness. "You're much easier to deal with when you're in a good mood."

He grunted his assent. "If you haven't given up on me yet, there's no place to go but up, Cait. Believe it or not, I do laugh and tease and generally get along with the rest of the human race."

She laughed. "You could have fooled me! But then, things around here are tense, and I know what it can do to the men."

Dominic's face was glistening with sweat, his golden eyes glowing with mirth. He took off his hard hat and wiped his forehead with the back of his bare arm. Cait felt his intense appraisal once again. A pulse leaped at the base of her throat. "You don't look scarred," he ventured.

"What?"

"Word gets around fast. I heard that you and Cirre locked horns earlier today. You must have won. I don't see any bruises or stabs in the back."

"Don't let the lack of wounds lead you into thinking he didn't get to me," she answered drily.

He nodded. "You do a good job of hiding it, then." He winked, gave the pickup a friendly pat and stepped away. "I'll have to remember that. Anyway, I owe you one."

Cait started the engine and shifted gears. "Oh?"

"For ordering the parts." His face sobered. "I won't

forget it, Cait. You're the first one who believed me enough to check on my complaints." He flashed her a sudden smile. "It's nice to know everyone doesn't think I'm the reason we're behind schedule."

As she guided the truck toward the office trailers, she felt giddy. He had used her first name. Why should she be so shocked? It rolled off his tongue like a deep purr from a contented cat.

Her mind spun with questions. Had Cirre deliberately made Dominic a scapegoat for his own ineffectuality? Had he then convinced Campos that the engineer was the culprit? That and Hank Parker's illness?

She entered her office floating. Somehow, seeing Dominic Tobbar just naturally made her feel good. Filipo hurried to meet her at the door with a pile of phone messages.

"Señor Louie Henning was able to get an earlier flight," he said, gesturing wildly. "He is waiting in BA, señora. Right now!"

"BA?" she echoed, puzzled.

Filipo shrugged eloquently. "Everyone refers to Buenos Aires as BA, señora."

"I see. Well, send a pilot to get him. I'm sure Louie won't mind waiting around for a couple of hours until someone gets there."

Filipo sighed dramatically. "But señora, the pilot has left for the eastern portion of the project. He is due in at San Luis in a few hours with a load of badly needed parts for the pipeline division."

Cait frowned and rubbed her chin in thought. There was a plane at the airstrip, but no pilot. "No flights in our direction from Ezezia?" she asked.

"None, señora. The pilot can make BA approximately eight hours from now," he finished lamely.

She stood up, pacing. That was too late. Louie must be exhausted from the flight, and she needed him in good working order by tomorrow morning. Suddenly she snapped her fingers. "Filipo, contact Señor Tobbar on the radio and ask him to get up here pronto."

Dominic Tobbar stuck his head in her office door fifteen minutes later. "Filipo said it was urgent."

Cait put down her pen. "Not urgent, but important. Can I collect on that favor you said you owed me?"

His eyes danced with silent laughter. "Sure. What do you have in mind?"

"A quick flight to BA. Right now."

"Business or personal?" he teased.

Cait returned his grin and picked up her hard hat. "Business. My cost controller just flew into BA, and I need him up here right away."

"Ah, I see. You intend to bolt his body to the records trailer early tomorrow morning, right?"

She laughed, following him out of the trailer and climbing into a truck. "How'd you guess?"

"You're quickly getting a reputation around here as Simon Legree, you know." He climbed into the driver's seat.

"I'll do anything short of selling my soul, to get this project back on schedule," she promised fervently.

He swung the truck out of the office area and headed toward the airstrip. A hot wind moved through the cab, for which Cait was thankful. Thinking of her appearance, she muttered a curse under her breath, and Tobbar cocked his head in her direction.

"What are you grousing about now?"

"Oh, nothing, really. I just wish I didn't have to go into Ezezia looking like a dust ball. All those gorgeously clad women in the terminal will die when they see me."

Dominic laughed. "Señora Monahan, believe me when I tell you you would put ninety percent of them to shame. Not many women can fill out a pair of jeans and a shirt so nicely."

She wasn't sure whether to protest, say thank you or get angry. Instead a blush stained her cheeks, and she closed her mouth, staring out the window, her pulse skipping erratically. She remained deep in thought for the two-hour flight to BA, using the time to sketch out several areas in which Louie Henning might want to begin investigating.

By keeping busy, Cait tried to ignore the powerful presence of Dominic, but in such close quarters she felt overwhelmed by him. Admittedly he was now more a friend than an adversary, Cait decided as she stared out the cockpit window. Still, she felt threatened by him.

Since landing in Argentina she had been immersed in her job. Not once, not until now, had she thought of Dave or their happy marriage. Her thick lashes swept down across her cheeks, and she felt the sting of hot tears. He would be proud of the job she was doing. A desperate longing filled her heart—she missed him. Now she had no one to tell her she was doing a good or bad job. She was in a position of authority that would cause men to silently hate her, yet she had no ally, no confidante. There was no Dave to sit down and talk to. . . .

"Got a headache?" Dominic inquired quietly.

Cait raised her head. "No—not really. A sort of one," she admitted.

"Damn lonely up on that perch, isn't it?"

She laughed softly, shaking her head. "Sometimes I'd rather be a turkey."

"An old American saying?"

She stretched languidly, like a cat awakening from a nap. "Yes. 'I'd rather soar with the eagles than fly with a bunch of turkeys.' Which means I'd rather do it alone than get fouled up with a bunch of aimless idiots."

His eyes danced. "Some days, it's safer to be a turkey. You can avoid people like Cirre. Right?"

She nodded, pulling out the pins that held her chignon in place. "True. I enjoy a challenging project like this, but it beats the hell out of my emotions."

"Welcome to the club, Cait." There was a longing look in his eyes as she unwound her captive tresses and allowed them to spill down over her left shoulder.

He reached out, sliding his fingers through her hair and sending a shiver of delight up her neck and shoulders. "You have the most beautiful hair. It's a shame you have to wear it up all the time." He had said it almost wistfully and then seemed to check himself, some of the unreadable mask slipping back over his features.

Shakily Cait brushed her hair, unable to find her voice. He did the most unexpected things at the most unexpected times. His touch had been so light, so gentle. She found herself wondering what it would be like to be loved by him. Abruptly she slammed the door on such ridiculous thoughts. What had come over her? she remonstrated herself silently.

Dominic gently banked the plane to the left, and Cait got her first real look at Ezezia Airport.

The sun hung low on the horizon, paving the dark blue-green Atlantic with a carpet of dappled orange and gold, reminding her of a brilliant Van Gogh painting. Dominic's touch, the yearning look in his eyes, seemed to have heightened her awareness of the world around her, and she leaned forward, gasping with delight at the colors spreading over the lush land comprising the southern edge of the Pampas. "It's lovely, Dominic," she said. "Any painter would revel in this sort of landscape. I never realized how beautiful your country is."

He smiled appreciatively, coaxing the Beechcraft into final landing position before approaching the runway. "A land so vast, so untamable that it will take your breath away," he promised.

A feeling of wonder flowed between them. As Cait sat back, watching him guide the plane, her vague thoughts and feelings crystalized. Dominic seemed to her like the untamed wildness of Argentina. A man of such inner strength coupled with primeval beauty and mysticism that it left her staring at him in awe— just as the land around her had made her stare in appreciative silence. He seemed to have cast a magic spell on her. He was like a wild jaguar, never quite tamed, always a threat. She couldn't label him, couldn't pin him down. He was a mystery.

She withdrew reluctantly from her introspection

and forced her thoughts back to the present. Once on the Miron Corporation landing apron, she assumed her professional self. She leaped easily to the ground from the wing and walked over to where Dominic was waiting for her. It felt good to let her long hair swing with the natural rhythm of her body, and she had a sudden inexplicable surge of undefined emotion.

"Louie!" she cried, running toward a stooped, balding man standing by the flight counter.

"Darlin'!" he chortled, taking her full weight as she flew into his arms.

Cait buried her head against his skinny neck, closing her eyes tightly against sudden tears. "Oh, God, Louie," she whispered. Images of Dave's death had surfaced once again. Louie had been on the platform at the time of the tragedy.

He patted her affectionately. "Hey, hey," he chided, "what's this? My Wild Irish Rose snifflin'? Come on, darlin', it's gonna be okay. Louie's here. Remember?"

They stood locked in a tight embrace. Louie rocked her slender body gently, murmuring endearments. He removed his wire-rim spectacles, his own eyes damp. "So let's take a look at you, gal," he ordered in a curiously high voice, holding her at arm's length.

Cait's face glistened with spilled tears, but she managed an embarrassed laugh, trying to wipe them away with the back of her hand. "Oh, Louie, you are a sight for sore eyes, believe me! You have no idea how glad I was when Goodell broke you loose from the Far East to help me out here." She stood on her tiptoes and planted a kiss on his cheek.

"Ahhh, you Irish are always full of blarney. You

ain't changed a bit, darlin'. Not a bit. Pretty as ever."

Her green eyes were bright with unabashed affection for him. She grasped his hand, squeezing it hard. "I'm—I'm so glad you're here," she whispered brokenly, tears glittering fiercely.

"I know, I know. It's been a long time coming back, has it?"

"Yes," she managed painfully. "I didn't realize how long, Louie."

He bowed his head, his thin mouth pursed. "A rotten piece of luck, darlin'. One in a million chance of happ'nin, believe me. But look, ole Louie, here, will bring some sunshine back in your life, and we'll make you smile like you used to out on those platforms. Remember how much fun we all had on P–31? The time we threw you overboard?" He chortled in fond remembrance, and Cait laughed with him.

Suddenly she remembered they were not alone. Reddening, she put her fingers to her lips at the gaffe and turned.

Dominic Tobbar's expression was hardened and attentive. His fiery, unspoken gaze met hers, and she felt more deeply embarrassed. He didn't understand. She and Louie were just good friends meeting once again. A cool smile tugged at one corner of his mouth as he walked over to them. He stood next to her, drinking in her upturned face, still wet with tears.

He removed a white handkerchief from his back pocket and placed it in her hand. "Wild Irish Rose," he murmured. "I'll have to remember that."

The stiffness of his voice was like acid on her tortured heart. She dabbed at her eyes and pulled her friend closer. "Louie, meet Dominic Tobbar. He leads up the bridge-building phase and was generous enough to be our pilot today."

Louie squinted, sizing up the civil engineer. He grasped Dominic's hand with his large-knuckled fingers. "From the tone in Cait's voice, I'd say she thinks very highly of you, Señor Tobbar. Thanks for coming down."

"Call me Dominic," he replied, giving Louie a firm handshake. He glanced at Cait, who was gradually pulling herself back together. "You must be very dear friends," he said in a voice tinged with sarcasm.

Louie grinned broadly, ignoring the innuendo, showing his crooked teeth. "The Rose and I go back seven years and many, many projects down the road. Ain't that right, darlin'?"

Cait frowned, perplexed by Dominic's attitude. "Many good times, Louie. Many," she answered, distracted.

"Are those your bags?" Dominic wanted to know, avoiding, Cait noticed, the intimate look that passed between her and Louie.

"Oh, yeah. I travel light. I hope like hell you got an interpreter at that site, Caitlin, my dear. I'm on the slats when it comes to Spanish."

Cait laughed throatily and hooked her arm through Louie's to lead him out of the terminal to the plane. "Don't worry, you'll know what they're saying even without an interpreter," she promised grimly.

The two-hour return flight seemed like fifteen minutes to Cait. Louie perched himself between their seats and told story after story. The cabin vibrated with good, healthy laughter, the sort of laughter that Cait knew would help heal still-tender wounds. She was acutely aware each time Dominic's gaze rested on her. Each time, she blushed. Something had happened between them...something intangible. She had not meant to cry, not meant to be so open about her feelings. Normally, she could cap them just as a drilling rig could cap an oil surge.

But Louie was more than a friend. He was like a father to her, and she would be eternally grateful for his care. New hope surged through her. Now that Louie was there, she would have at least one ally.

After landing back at the Rio Colorado, Dominic excused himself. Cait told Pedro where to put the baggage and ran to catch up.

"Dominic!" she called breathlessly, coming to a halt as he turned. She could barely make out his features in the darkness. "Thanks for taking time out of your schedule. I—"

"No need for thanks. I'll do it when you need me, Cait." He smiled absently, resting his hands on his narrow hips. "That's a good name for you, you know. Wild Irish Rose. A lovely red rose with thorns."

She smiled simply, unable to meet his eyes. "I'm afraid all you've seen since I've been here is my thorny side."

He shook his head. "No. You're a woman of many, many facets. I've just been privileged to see another side of you."

She folded her arms against her chest. "Oh, yes, the crybaby side. It doesn't happen often. Louie was..." She halted, biting her lower lip. "He was on the gas platform when the accident occurred. If—if it hadn't been for him, Dominic, I'd never have been able to pull myself together afterward." She shrugged painfully and managed a broken smile. "You see, that's why I cried today at the airport. He brought back so many memories...but good ones too. He stood by me when I needed someone."

Dominic seemed to lose some of his surliness, the harsh lines of his face softening with understanding. "I see," he murmured, looking down at her. "You're lucky you have people like that who care deeply for you."

She gave him a questioning glance. "Surely you do too? No one can go through life alone. We all need someone sometime..." Her voice trailed off as she saw his features harden once again.

"The only kind of women I know are heartless ones. I'm afraid my experiences differ greatly from your own."

Cait shook her head. She wanted to stop the coldness growing between them. She wanted to confide in him, wanted him to confide in her. "But family...your mother or father must have provided you with that sort of emotional support—"

He inhaled deeply and stepped back into the shadows. "My mother died when I was five, and my father only wanted me to follow family tradition by becoming a surgeon. Instead I became the black sheep of the family." He stared defiantly into the Patagonian night. "You see that Scottish gorse growing out there on the sides of those barren hills, Cait?"

"Yes?" she almost whispered.

"I'm like that brush, starved for water, grown wild and tough in order to survive. I kick around Argentina just like that brush is pushed by the winds of the Andes along this desert region." His stormy eyes clouded. "Maybe that's why I find you so refreshing, so different. You respond openly to other people's emotions. Maybe I'm jealous of your relationship with Louie. I'd like to share that—" Without finishing the sentence he turned and stalked away, leaving her standing alone in the darkness. She could almost hear the unspoken words: "I would like to share that *with you.*"

Chapter Five

As IF TO HERALD the difficult day ahead, the sun at dawn was blood red. Its long, searching rays warmed the cold land slowly.

Over her first cup of coffee Cait sat with Louie Henning and Campos, who sipped maté. Their heads bowed, they were studying several sheets of facts and figures that Cait had gathered together. The Argentinian tapped the sum total at the bottom of the last page. "In my estimation, Señor Henning—"

"Call me Louie," the other man growled, punching a new set of numbers into his calculator.

Campos cleared his throat nervously. "Sí, Louie. The fact sheets . . . they show a slow decline that is due to Señor Parker's illness." His voice became colored with feeling as he added, "Plus the union problems."

Cait watched the cost controller through partly-lowered lashes. It was as if Campos hadn't even spoken. She could always tell when Louie had discovered something wrong. His brow furrowed like neat rows of tilled soil. The silence lengthened in the office, and

Campos cleared his throat twice more, then rose to get a second cup of maté.

"Cait, darlin', do me a favor."

"Sure, Louie."

"Roust those supers out of their bunks early this morning. I want to talk to each and every one of them. I need a basic overlay from each department before I can match figures to reasons."

Cait glanced over at Campos. "Jorge, will you get in touch with them?"

"Sí. Of course. I'll call them right away."

They watched Campos disappear into the next office. Louie nudged Cait and motioned toward his scribbled figures. "That ain't no three-month decline, darlin'," he muttered. "Somethin's wrong."

"You always did have a nose for trouble."

"And didn't you think his reasons were weak?" Louie challenged.

Cait shrugged, sipping the coffee. "Call it a hunch . . . maybe nothing more than that. Cirre has been defensive. Jorge has been helpful, if a little prejudiced."

Louie fluffed the stack of papers together with finality. "In what way?"

"Toward Dominic." Cait surprised herself by using his first name in such a casual manner. But Louie was a friend and she felt she could drop her managerial pretense with him.

"He's a leader," Louie stated flatly.

"Yes. Also someone who questions orders or raises hell when his end of the project isn't being supplied properly."

Henning's thin eyebrows moved upward. "The trouble goes back to our purchasing fella, Cirre, doesn't it?"

"Looks like it. The replacement crane sheaves were ordered six months ago, and were placed on back order twice. We just ordered more from an outside supplier. They'll arrive by truck in two days. Plus, much of the equipment around here seems to be machinery bought second hand."

Louie grimaced. "We're off to a bad start to begin with, then. As my old granny used to say: new project, new machinery. That way, equipment is insured and under warranty, and in the long run it costs less to maintain and run."

Cait grinned. "You had a smart old granny."

Louie chortled. "Irish grandmas ain't too bad either, darlin'."

She groaned. "I don't know. This job may be the death of me yet!"

"Ah, darlin', in this job, like all the rest, you need a lot of bull to soothe ruffled feathers. Some call it diplomacy." He lost his elfin smile. "You seem to think a lot of this Tobbar fellow. Would he level with me if I pulled him aside and asked his version of what's going on at the site? Unofficially, that is."

Cait leaned back, deep in thought. She wanted to blurt out that of course Dominic was trustworthy. But did she really know that? He'd been involved in every major squabble that had arisen on the site since she had arrived. Only recently she had mollified him by ordering the crane parts. It was funny how something so insignificant could tame the most ferocious jaguar.

Louie squinted at her. "Give me your gut feeling," he demanded.

"Yes. I trust him. But he's damn touchy and overly sensitive. I don't know if he'd cooperate with you, me or anyone. All he wants is to build that bridge and bring it in on time."

"Can't blame a guy for that, darlin'. You know how some civils get when things go badly—even if it ain't their fault."

She shook her head, frowning. "That's just it, Louie. Cirre, Campos and some of the union stewards are all saying he's responsible for the delays. I can't disprove it at this point, but the evidence is in his favor." She gave him a troubled look. "That's why I needed you down here. I don't have time to sort out this mess, but I need to know who I can trust. If you can weed out the troublemakers, I can slot them into a powerless position and we can move this project forward."

Henning smiled sympathetically and patted her arm. "Leave the investigation to me. In two days or so, we'll have some concrete answers. Don't forget about that big-wig conference in BA on Monday," he reminded her. "I'm aiming to have the bulk of the research done by then so you can take substantial evidence with you."

She grimaced. "God, I've been trying to forget about that! All the top Miron officials are going to be there for our progress report." She rose, running her hand across her hair in a distracted motion.

"Who's going from here?"

"Campos, Cirre and myself. They're leaving tomorrow night. I'm flying into BA late Sunday evening."

"Don't you want to fly in Friday night with them and get a taste of the city?"

"I'd love to, but I have work to do."

Henning shrugged his shoulders. "The way Tobbar looks at you, I'd say let him take you in some weekend, darlin'. Never know, you might have a better time than you thought."

Cait stared. "What? Louie, what on earth prompted you to say that?"

"I'm fifty-nine years old, my wild Irish rose, and I saw the look in his eye. The man definitely has an interest in you . . . or haven't you noticed?" he drawled.

Her heart thumped once, as if to underscore Louie's observation. It was true. She felt more alive when Dominic was around. She saw a world of color and vibrancy that she thought had died with Dave. Dominic made her feel good about life again, and she looked forward to their next meeting. Still, she wasn't ready to acknowledge her feelings to anyone but herself. Louie's grin infuriated her, and she placed her hands belligerently on her hips. "You must be seeing things."

He laughed. "Maybe you don't want to see the truth, darlin'. But, as always, you look lovely when you blush."

She joined in his laughter. "Louie, I don't know why you never married. You do a girl so much good. Flattery will get you everywhere with me." Some of her merriment fled. "And to tell the truth, I can use some right now," she admitted softly.

He nodded, gauging her keenly. "Let the past go, Rose," he returned quietly.

"What?"

"Darlin', you're still carryin' a torch for Dave. He's gone, and you gotta put the past behind you."

An aching lump formed in her throat, and she tried to swallow. It felt as if a knife were scoring her heart. Hot, scalding tears crowded in her eyes, and she compressed her lips to fight back from crying openly. "Damn you, Louie Henning," she whispered painfully.

"I love you enough to be honest, darlin'." He walked over, slipping his arm around her shoulders and giving her a quick hug. "You're a team person, Cait. Being out of marriage is like being the only pony in a two-horse hitch."

"I suppose you expect me to jump right back in?" she demanded.

"No need to be angry, darlin'. I'm just sayin' to open your eyes a little and notice the signals that men are giving you, that's all. I didn't say you had to marry the first fella that comes along. But at least get back in the water. Don't stand on the shore and watch life pass you by." He waved his finger at her as he halted at the door. "There's nothing written that says a second marriage can't be as good as or better than the first. Remember that."

She managed a small smile. "One of your granny's old sayings?"

Henning grinned. "That i' tis, darlin'. Well, I'm off to play the inquisitor to your supers. I'll tag you at lunchtime."

Only some of Cait's irritation had faded by the

time Henning walked into her office near noon. It was hot and sticky and she was pacing like a caged cat. She was still upset over another confrontation with Campos earlier that morning. "Let's take a ride down to the river, darlin', and get you out of this hot box," he suggested.

Grabbing her hard hat and bag lunch, she followed him without a word. As she drove toward the inviting Rio Colorado, she began to calm down.

"Well, did you drop the ax?" Louie asked.

"Yes. Campos was screaming." Cait blew out a long breath. "God, Louie, I don't know if I'm up to all this."

"You're doin' fine, Rose. This site only needs two shifts, not three. We both know that."

"Not according to Jorge. Good Lord, he was saying all the unions will strike in protest and—"

"They got no basis for a strike. The contract covers shift work." Henning waved his finger at her. "It specifically states that management has the power to decide how many shifts. So quit being a worry-wart." He grinned. "Ah, this is a lovely area, isn't it?"

For the first time she noticed the lush line of tropical plants and trees that graced the river bank. Pulling the truck to a halt near the bridge-building operations, they got out and padded through the dust to a shady eucalyptus tree. Cait sat down with a flop, threw off the hard hat and leaned back against the rough bark, closing her eyes. New sounds, soothing sounds, invaded her tense body. The chirp of the ever-present hornero, a bird common to the area, erased Campos's screaming from her mind. The gentle breeze dried the perspiration that made her shirt cling to her body.

"Here, you need to eat, darlin'. You're gettin' too skinny."

Cait took the peanut-butter sandwich he offered, and reluctantly sat up, scanning the dappled sunlit river that moved past them like a silent blue-green ribbon. "It's so peaceful," she whispered.

"That i' tis," Henning agreed, biting hungrily into his sandwich.

She tasted hers and made a face. "I'm not hungry, Louie . . ."

"Eat it anyway. You're just upset right now. You still need food. Especially under these conditions, darlin'." He winked.

Cait concentrated on eating.

"Well, look who's comin'." Henning waved and motioned toward Dominic Tobbar, who had just climbed out of his truck.

The peanut butter stuck in her throat, and Cait couldn't swallow for a moment. She stared openly as Dominic walked easily toward them. The fluid grace of his body reminded her again of a stalking jaguar. His shirt sleeves were rolled high on his arms, the vee open at the throat, displaying the column of his neck and tendrils of black hair. She swallowed convulsively as he joined them under the tree. Her heart was hammering, and she was thoroughly irritated with herself at her silly reaction. Frowning, she barely acknowledged his nod.

"Glad you could join us," Henning was saying equably.

Dominic dug in his own brown paper bag and pulled out three sandwiches. Cait stared down at them. He offered one to her.

"Uh, no," she stammered, feeling a blush sweep across her neck and into her face.

"He's still growin', Cait," Louie said with a laugh.

"I guess," she growled, sitting back and trying to ignore both of them. Damn Louie, she thought. The peace she had so desperately wanted was shattered.

Cait gazed longingly back at the river to try to recapture the feeling. But she was too aware of Dominic's friendly appraisal. His eyes were now pale, cinnamon brown, and she found herself mesmerized by his expression. Slowly she relaxed beneath his warming gaze.

All too soon, Louie rose, dusting off his pants. "Well, I forgot I've set a twelve-fifteen appointment. I'll see you later."

"Louie!" Cait shot him a stricken look.

"Now, darlin', Dominic will keep you company while I'm gone."

She gritted her teeth, glaring up at the controller. "I'm going to shoot you, Louie Henning, when I get you alone," she promised.

He was gone far too quickly for her, and she nervously dug in the sack for the fruit. It turned out to be an orange, and she peeled it savagely.

"Bad morning?" Dominic asked.

"If you must know, yes."

"Anything I can do to make it go better?"

She felt compelled to talk, but also giddy—and afraid. Actually, she shouldn't discuss her job with him, another employee. But since when had Dominic ever acted in that capacity? As Louie emphatically stated, he was a leader in every sense of the word, and that thought inspired Cait to confide in him.

"Oh, that damn Campos is such a crybaby. You'd think I'd just cut off his right hand, by canceling the third shift this morning. Good Lord!"

"You cut third?"

"Yes. It had to be done. They weren't making up the time differential."

Dominic stretched out in front of her like a large cat after a meal. He chewed on a sprig of grass. "That was Campos's idea, you know. To put in a third shift."

"Yes. Don't I know it." Her nostrils flared with anger. "Dominic, I just wish everyone in supervisory capacity could act like adults instead of children. It's so infuriating, and it takes every last ounce of my patience to remain cool."

He smiled lazily, studying her through his thick dark lashes. "I finally see where you put that Irish temper of yours," he teased.

Cait met his gaze, caressed by the unspoken message it conveyed, then gave a little laugh of self-defeat. "You haven't seen anything yet. There have been times when I've had to leave a site, drive into the jungle or along some deserted beach and just scream."

"Let me know when you need to do that and I'll come along and scream with you."

She sobered. "Yes, I'm sure you've got some bottled-up anger too."

He shrugged his broad shoulders. "It's nice to know I'm not alone." He rose to his feet and held out his hand. "Come on, I want to show you something."

Cait stared at him open-mouthed. His fingers were long, and there were thick calluses on his palms. She shocked herself by allowing her hand to fall into his.

His fingers closed firmly about her flesh, the contact so electrifying that she scarcely felt herself being pulled effortlessly upward. Memories of Dave's touch, of his gentle strength, flowed poignantly to the surface. Reluctantly she pulled her hand free and stood only inches away from Dominic's masculine body. An inner part of her seemed to melt, and she felt breathless. She followed him hesitantly toward the river.

They walked to the lip of the Rio Colorado and past where the cofferdams were being constructed. The crane stood silent on the barge, looking like a gawky sentinel. Cait stepped carefully across the vines, over tree limbs that had grown old and fallen to the mossy earth, and kept an eye out for snakes. They moved upriver for what seemed only a few minutes. The gray hornero darted swiftly between the cascading arms of the silver-leafed eucalyptus, calling melodically. Cait wondered if the bird was announcing their entrance into some magical realm. Her excitement rose, and she relished the physical exercise, her hand still tingling from the brief caress of Dominic's fingers.

They breasted a small rise, and she gasped with pleasure as her gaze swept across a small crescent-shaped cove that seemed to belong to another world. Large cypress trees swathed in light-green moss hung over the edges of the black sand beach like nurturing guardians. The water was a crystal-clear blue. Tropical birds filled the air with vibrant color and melodious song. Dominic looked at her with an enigmatic smile.

"Well, what do you think?"

"It's lovely," she breathed. "So lovely. Oh, Dominic, this is incredible!"

Without a word, he led her down a narrow path that led to the secluded area. Cait stopped at the foot of the path, enchanted by the cove. Her eyes shimmered with appreciation, and she inhaled the tangy scent of the mango and orange trees that dotted the landscape. Dominic stood watching her. Finally she faced him, opening her hands in a helpless gesture. "It's so . . . healing . . ."

"I call it Bahía Linda. Lovely bay."

She knelt down on the black sand and ran her fingers across the warm, grainy texture. "It's a small garden of Eden."

He stood near her, resting his hands on his hips and gazing out at the river that moved sluggishly beyond the protected arm of the cove. "It's yours, to come here when you want to get away from it all. BA is too far, but this is close enough to just sit down to think or mull over troublesome situations."

Cait gazed up at him. His figure blocked out the probing rays of the tropical sun, and the rugged outline of his brow, nose and jaw conveyed his strength. "Do you need this place sometimes?" she ventured.

He looked down with a wry smile. "Many times. Especially when Campos and Cirre start playing games."

She moved her arm in an encompassing gesture. "I never thought you would be the type to need—"

"Oh, I need, all right." His eyes became a darker gold. "I can take a lot, but after a while I get beaten down, just like everyone else."

She sifted the sand through her fingers, perplexed, yet compelled to explore him further. "Is there anyone you can go to, confide in?"

His mouth tightened and his stance grew rigid as he stared out at the Rio Colorado. "No."

She folded her hands against her knees, sensing his withdrawal. "Is—is that why you were angry with me the other night when we came back from BA?"

"Angry?" His hands fell from his hips and he turned to look down at her upturned face. "No," he said gently, "I wasn't angry. Maybe..." he shrugged. "Jealous, perhaps."

"You, jealous?"

"I envy your ability to be warm and open. It's obvious that Louie loves you dearly, as you do him. It's touching to see that sort of relationship."

Shivering at the caressing purr in his voice, Cait murmured, "Anyone can have friends. Good friends, who are like family to you."

He smiled grimly. "You are naive after all," he teased.

Cait bristled, getting to her feet. "At twenty-nine, I'm hardly naive!"

His mouth curved absently. "I'm beginning to see a side to you that is and always will be a child. Now, that's not an insult, so don't get upset."

She stood only inches from him, her anger receding quickly within his magnetic presence. His expression grew serious, and he reached out, stroking her flushed cheek where tendrils of loosened hair had curled in the humidity. She quivered at his touch.

"Did you know you're like that lagoon over there?" he whispered huskily, his thumb tracing her jaw line.

"I love to watch your face when you get excited or upset. It's so transparent, so incredible . . ."

Cait closed her eyes as he traced a trail of fire with his thumb. Her heart beat erratically while his fingers caressed the curve of her neck, resting finally on her shoulder.

"Every ripple, every emotion is like a pebble thrown into the water. You mirror each feeling. You're like a peaceful pool in tune with everything around you." He studied her intently, staring at her parted full lips. Reluctantly he removed his hand from her shoulder. "I promised to be on my best behavior with you, so we'd better get back, or I won't be held accountable." He made a half turn, gesturing around the bay. "Consider Bahía Linda yours, Cait, and come here whenever you want to. This is a place to dream of the past and the future, a healing place."

She had barely breathed during the past few seconds, acutely aware of where his hand had been. Somehow she found her voice, slightly husky with breathlessness. "Why not wish for things in the present?"

He shrugged, his eyes twinkling. "That's not a bad idea either. Never think about the past, because it's gone. The future is nothing more than tomorrow's present."

She shook her head, savoring his closeness and his male scent. "We make our future by working in the present."

His smile disappeared, and a molten gold came to his eyes as he regarded her slender figure. "I've never been so aware of the present as I am this moment," he murmured.

A thrill of joy burst within her, but she could only nod mutely, lost within his warming look.

They walked back in a shared silence. She was acutely aware of the closeness of his male body, the immense power that seemed to be held in tight control. He was like a jaguar ready to spring. Her thoughts turned back to their last moments of conversation. He had stood like a bulwark of solitude. She wanted to reach out to him, to share some of that undefinable weight of responsibility he seemed to carry.

Chapter Six

It was close to midnight before Cait finished the report she was working on and went to bed. Dominic and Louie were working late too, but they'd promised to wake her if they discovered anything important.

She slept restlessly, dreaming of Dominic. She had sensed a new eagerness in him to share with her. In her dream, they were at Bahía Linda, and she was walking happily along the beach by his side. The balm of peace drove her into a deeper, more restful phase of sleep, and she saw herself sitting on the beach alone, warming in the rays of the sun.

A familiar voice began calling her. Her heart began to thump wildly, and suddenly she found herself back on the drilling platform. She groaned, tossing restlessly. She didn't want to be back on that gas rig. Dave and his crew were working down below. The crane boom swung a load of steel I-beams lazily through the air, toward the center of the new platform.

Cait whimpered, feeling her hands grow moist with perspiration. A black tidal wave of fear engulfed her seconds before the crane cable snapped. She stood paralyzed, watching the tons of steel begin to fall. She wanted to shout, to warn them. My God!

Chaos was everywhere! Men on the platform bellowing orders...her anguished voice...the trapped men shrieking among the wreckage. She tried to get closer, but hands closed firmly around her arms, pulling her back.

"No...let me go...Dave! Help—"

"Cait! Wake up!"

Her voice was raw, gutted with pain, as she suddenly awakened from the clutches of the nightmare. Her breath came in sharp sobs, her hair swirling in wild disarray around her tear-stained cheeks. Dominic's face loomed before her, and she gave a small whimper of relief as his arms slid around her in a tentative embrace. She trembled within his grasp, burying her head against his shoulder, crying wildly as scattered images began to dissolve into the recesses of her memory.

"Sshh," he soothed, stroking her hair with a gentle motion. "It's all right, *querida*. Sshh, it's all over. No more nightmares. That's it, relax, you're safe..."

His voice, healing balm to her frayed emotions, assuaged her pain. She clutched tightly at his shirt front, her tears thoroughly wetting the rough fabric. It seemed forever until she could rest, quiet and subdued, against his strong, supportive body. Gradually she became aware of his fingers stroking her unbound hair, and she opened her eyes, releasing a long sigh.

The strong beat of his heart was slow, rhythmic and even, not wildly thumping like her own. Gradually she felt him relaxing, pulling her deeper into his arms. He held her tightly as she continued to tremble.

His hand trailed down the flowing length of her hair, sliding onto the apricot gown and coming to rest near her waist.

Cait became aware of the altered pressure of his fingers as he gently began to massage her tightly corded back muscles. A feeling of utter warmth flowed through her with each ministration, and she lay silently against him, her eyes still tightly shut. A new sensation, more electrifying and disturbing, coursed through her, and she felt Dominic respond almost immediately. His work-roughened hand slid around her torso, caressing the side of her breast and then moving downward, following the natural curve of her flat stomach and rounded hip. His breath became ragged, and Cait listened as the tempo of his heart leaped upward with the pulsing of her own.

Guilessly she strained against his hard chest, mindlessly following her unconscious need. A new ache throbbed through her, and she gave a moan of pleasure as his hand once again caressed her breast. The skin grew taut, crying to be touched and tamed beneath his demanding fingers.

Cait heard him groan and felt his hand closing about her arms, moving her away from the security of his body. "No," she heard him growl softly. "Not this way, Cait...not now...*Dios,* how I want you..."

Hurt and rejection filled her as she looked up into his mobile features. The gray dawn softened the harsh lines of his face, and he tilted his head, silently studying her. The fiery gold of his eyes spoke of his desire, of the hunger that was becoming overwhelming, that only she could satisfy. He swore softly.

"I've never had to take care of a woman who was genuinely hurt...who...I don't think it's right to take advantage of a situation..." He shook his head, his fingers trailing across her wet cheeks. "You're like a lost child...so damn vulnerable...hurting..." His voice dropped into a husky whisper as he pulled her back into his arms, cradling her head against his neck and jaw. His arms tightened about her momentarily, and he brushed her damp forehead with a kiss. "I thought I knew everything there was to know about women." He gave a low, throaty chuckle. "At thirty-five, it's disconcerting as hell to realize I don't."

The remnants of her nightmare were gradually evaporating. She clung wordlessly to him, not understanding much of what he said but responding to the timbre of his raw voice. She shivered, acutely aware of the honesty and care in his tone. It said so much more than the actual words. A flicker of hope flared within her, and she sat up, reaching out to touch his unshaven face.

"I'm just glad you're here," she murmured brokenly. "You have no idea how happy I am you came."

"It was sheer luck that I did come," he told her.

Dazed by the nightmare, Cait looked groggily around. "What time is it?"

"Five-thirty."

She pulled her hand free and rubbed her face wearily. "God, did you hear me screaming, clear from the offices?"

His voice was softened. "No. Louie sent me over to get you. I guess I came right in the middle of it. When I pulled up outside your quarters and heard your screams, I thought someone was attacking you. I came barging in here and found you in a tangle of sheets and blankets."

She let her hands drop in her lap and licked her dry, chapped lips. "Do me a favor?"

"Name it."

"Make me some coffee."

"Will you be all right here by yourself?"

"Yes . . . no . . ." Her voice cracked, and she buried her face in her hands.

"Take your time," he coaxed huskily.

Just the light touch of his hand sliding down the length of her hair calmed the uncontrolled fear still raging within her. Her hands shook slightly when she tried to wipe away the cascading tears. When had she ever cried so much? Or had she been holding the tears in all this time and never known it . . . not until now?

Dominic slipped a fresh Kleenex into her hands, and she mumbled her thanks, dabbing at her eyes. She sat with her shoulders hunched forward, head hanging down, dark sheets of hair hiding her tortured face. How could she explain something so personal and painful to him? Yet she knew he was already helping her. There was no questioning look in his glance . . . only acceptance of her pain.

"I'm sorry, Dominic . . ."

"For what? Being human doesn't require an apology, querida." A tender flame burned in his golden eyes as he watched her gravely. "You're teaching me something of great value. Maybe sharing pain is best."

"Maybe you're right," she whispered hoarsely.

His hand slid along her shoulder in a kneading motion. "How about that coffee now?"

She nodded, sniffling and then blowing her nose.

She felt his weight lift from the bed.

She got up too, and dressed in slow, uncoordinated movements. The familiar sounds of coffee perking and boots sounding on the uncarpeted floor made her feel better. Running a brush through her long hair, she finally joined him in the other room. He was standing by the heating element, his arms crossed, his expression grim.

She busied herself wiping the two ceramic mugs free of the perpetual dust and set them on the makeshift table fashioned from surplus lumber. He was watching her closely, but this time his gaze did not irritate her.

"Do you get those nightmares often?" he asked.

"Yes." She sat down on one of the stools and motioned for him to join her after he poured the coffee. Trying to ignore the growing tension between them, she concentrated on putting sugar and powdered milk in her cup.

"Maybe . . ." She sounded peevish. Frowning, she took a sip and set the cup down. "I'm sorry. I shouldn't be so damn crabby."

"It's understandable." His voice was coaxing, soothing. "You're still working through the trauma, Cait."

An invisible anvil of grief descended upon her heart, and she sighed heavily, staring down at the cup. Her lower lip trembled, and she tucked it between her teeth, fighting off another wave of tears.

"Oh, God . . . I wish the dreams would end! I don't understand why I still get them. It's been over a year . . ." She closed her eyes for a moment and caressed the cup in a slow motion. She faltered, giving Dominic a vulnerable, helpless look. "Why am I sitting here telling you all this? You don't need to know my personal problems. You have enough of your own here on the site without adding mine to the list."

He smiled wryly. "I don't mind. I usually handle my emotions by ignoring them, but that doesn't really work. I like your way of dealing with them better. That's why, if you feel like it, you should talk this thing out. Maybe it would make the nightmares go away."

"It's funny," she murmured. "I've never talked about this to anyone. Not even Louie."

"Tell me about it."

"After I married Dave..." She swallowed hard, her eyes glittering with pent-up tears. "We hop-scotched around the Far East, setting up gas drilling platforms and laying pipe."

"Did you enjoy that kind of life?" he probed.

"Very much." Her face took on a more animated quality. "Every platform was a new challenge, and we worked well as a team..." Her voice took on a dreamier tone, and her face, a faraway look. She almost forgot he was listening.

"Dave had a knack for the technical problems, and I was good at scheduling. Brentworth would throw us the deadbeat platforms that were behind, and we'd work out a plan on how to get them back on their feet and in on time. It was a big game, and we had so much fun." Her emerald eyes cleared as she looked at him. "Dave taught me that a good sense of humor is like a plating of armor." She whispered, "God, I need a sense of humor now, more than ever."

"Everyone should allow himself a few moments of peace and laughter. I don't think you've spent your quota on yourself, so go ahead and use them up."

"You sound like Louie, dammit." She was suddenly angry.

"He's a wise man."

"And I suppose you follow his advice?" she returned acidly.

Dominic smiled patiently. "No. But let's just say that between you and his wisdom, I'm learning a lot of new and helpful ways to vent my buried frustration and anger. You're teaching me, and I'm grateful for the experience, although"—he reached out to squeeze her hand—"I would never wish you any pain like what I'm seeing you go through. Dios, it tears me up..."

Cait felt her anger dissipate with the pressure of his fingers against her own. She was at a loss for words, and, hearing the searching, questioning tone of his voice, it struck her that he had probably never known a woman like herself, someone who openly shared her feelings and emotions.

"What you need, Cait, is to take some time off from this site and relax," Dominic continued. "Louie told me you've been pushing hard ever since your husband's death. Even I know you can't run from grief. It has to be faced squarely. The sooner the better."

She got up, a troubled frown on her brow. "Relax and do what?"

"There's a world out there that I think you'd enjoy." He stood up too, and put his cup over by the heating element. "Sometime, when you're ready, I'll take you to BA and show you a city of great beauty. Is it a deal?"

She chewed on her lower lip, watching him through

her lashes. She wanted to tell him how much she owed him. She had not forgotten the strength of his arms around her as she had sobbed out her grief and pain. But a small fear kept nagging at her, and she couldn't understand the feeling. "I'll think about it," she promised softly. "We'd better get over to the records office, or Louie will think we've gotten lost."

Before they left the truck to go into the records trailer, Cait reached out. It was the first time she had deliberately touched his arm, and she felt the warmth and hardness of his muscles beneath her fingertips.

"Thanks," she said in a hushed tone. "For being there."

"I'll be there again if you need me, Cait. Just remember that."

Louie looked up as they entered the trailer. His gaze settled on Cait, and his frown deepened. "You look like hell."

"Go easy on her," Dominic warned, a growl in his voice.

Cait's eyes widened briefly. For the second time in twelve months she felt she had a protector. She patted Louie on the shoulder. "It's all right, Louie. Dominic had the misfortune of walking in when I was having my usual nightmare."

"You okay, darlin'?"

"Yes, fine. He makes a good cup of coffee. Did you know that?"

Louie grinned. "I knew Tobbar was good for something. You feel up to all this, or not?"

Cait sat down opposite Louie and watched Dominic pull up another chair. "I have to be. Did you two stay up all night?"

"Don't we look it, Rose?"

"No. I look worse than both of you combined, and I supposedly got some sleep." She laughed.

The controller made a face and laid eleven bills of lading out neatly in front of her. "This problem is much larger than we anticipated, darlin'. Not only are some of the materials not reaching the site, but what is reaching the site is being overbilled."

"Such as?"

"Dom was kind enough to prowl around early this morning and do some weighing and counting for me— petrol levels, acetyline, and about eight other assorted items. He counted what we really have, against what we supposedly received and used. In every instance, there was less than what was tallied on the store-keeper's inventory sheets."

Cait pressed her lips together. "So what's your final analysis, Louie?"

"To keep this kind of systematic kickback going, someone needs to keep a very good set of records. Our friend Cirre has probably got another set of books with the real figures. Do you see the implications of all this?"

She sought Dominic's face and saw his agreement. "What kind of money are we talking so far, Louie?"

"If these eleven items are projected over the previous year, I would say at least six hundred thousand dollars. Is that enough to take to BA with you in your report?"

The pit of her stomach knotted. "Damn," Cait whispered. She gritted her teeth at the thought of the long-range implications. How could Hank Parker let something like this go undetected? Or—she gasped, turning to Louie. "You aren't saying Campos covered this whole thing up, are you?"

The silence became almost tangible as she looked from Louie to Dominic and back again. Getting to her feet, she began to pace, unable to sit still any longer. Campos was a trusted site supervisor . . . but only he could get away with so much pilferage . . . so much excess materials.

Finally Louie broke the silence.

"Hank Parker was no dummy, darlin'. He had to be very sick most of the time not to notice that Campos was gradually weaning control away from him. Look at this. Eighty-five percent of the invoices are signed by Campos, starting about a year ago. Materials invoices should have been signed by Hank. We've dug far enough back in the records to show the gradual take-over by Campos."

Louie brought forward another handful of reports and placed them in front of her. "Campos hated Dom, here, because he reported, in writing, all the problems. As you can see, none of these reports has been initialed by Hank, so he never saw them and couldn't act on the problem. Campos very conveniently kept them in the bottom drawer of his desk, under lock and key." Louie allowed himself a small smile of satisfaction. "I'm still a fairly decent lock-picker when I want to be, darlin'."

She sat down, stunned. She had handled time or flow problems, but never a managerial cover-up. "What we need," she muttered, "is that second set of records. I can't go into that meeting with a few scraps of evidence, Louie. I'll get laughed out of there, and you know it."

He nodded sagely. "We've already discussed that, Rose. Now, calm down. You look as white as a sheet. Are you sure you're all right?"

Cait rubbed her face tiredly. "I'm fine."

"As I was saying, Dom and I have a solution to your problem."

"To call in Cirre?" she asked.

"He and Campos left late last night for BA. Dom thinks we'll find that book in Cirre's city apartment. I already went through the storekeeper's desk, and anything else that was locked, and didn't find a thing. He's slick."

"I can't just walk up to Cirre and demand the book," Cait said.

"You won't have to," Dominic interrupted. "The three of us will fly into BA today and pay him a visit."

A shiver of fear rippled up her spine. His voice was laced with hatred. She had never seen Dominic look as threatening as he did now. Not even at the print shack had she seen that awful light of anger in his dark eyes. "And if he doesn't talk?"

"He will," Dominic promised.

Chapter Seven

CAIT HAD FORGOTTEN what hot water, steam and loads of creamy soap could do to her body. Finally, in the luxury of the company-rented apartment in Buenos Aires, she was able to wash away the Patagonian dust. Tiredness began to seep into her as she turned slowly under the pummeling streams that kneaded her tense muscles. She finally emerged from the bathroom, wrapped in a thick terry-cloth robe, with a towel wrapped around her head. Unable to resist the tempting queen-size bed, she stretched out on the vibrant copper spread. Her eyes closed almost as soon as her head sank into the pillow.

Cait awoke with a start, sat up and stared around the dusky room. Silence greeted her except for the faint honk of a horn on some distant *avenida*. The towel about her head had loosened, and someone had covered her with a blanket. Her hair spilled across her shoulders as she lurched to her feet and padded into the quiet living room. She spotted a note on the coffee table and sat down on the sofa to read it: "Darlin', you looked too beautiful to wake up. Dom and I went to find Cirre. We'll be back when we find what we're looking for. Love, Louie."

"Damn him," she whispered, letting the note drop to the sofa. Gazing forlornly about the room, she realized that this was one of the few times she had slept without dreaming at all. She felt almost human now. Glancing at her watch, she calculated that she had slept five or six hours.

Cait stepped out on the black, wrought-iron balcony, where lingering twilight gilded the horizon in a wash of soft peach. Buenos Aires was a city of lights. Along Avenida Alvear, winking, blinking floodlights illuminated beautifully sculpted buildings standing like miniature palaces from the days of Louis XV. Inhaling deeply, Cait detected a faint scent of oranges in the air. A slight breeze caressed her face and a sad smile pulled at her lips. BA was romantic, a subtle lover weaving his spell. A new excitement threaded through her. She was anxious to explore the vast cosmopolitan city.

A knock on the door startled Cait, and she drew in a sharp breath. Her heart leaped as she rose to open it. It was Dominic.

"Where's Louie?" she asked, her voice husky.

"Over at the Claridge House," he answered, quickly perusing her with his dark eyes. He held out a thick maroon book.

Their eyes met and she shivered, sensing the tightly coiled anger in him ready to explode. Biting her lip, she opened the book and studied the figures, then followed him into the living room.

"It must have been bad," she ventured, sitting down.

He poured a shot of whiskey into a crystal glass. Cait colored, realizing her silk bathrobe clung to the rounded curves of her body. "Somewhat," he drawled, making himself comfortable opposite her on the sofa.

"Is Louie all right?" she asked, her eyes mirroring the sudden uncertainty she was feeling.

Dominic's stony features softened. "He's tired right now. It took a long time to track Cirre down, and Louie was prettty beat by the time we finished." He managed a sour smile and took closer note of Cait. "I'm glad we decided to let you sleep."

She frowned. "When I woke up, I was angry," she admitted. "But this is the first time I've really slept well, and I needed it."

"Once we found Cirre, it took another hour to persuade him to give us the book."

"As simple as that?" Cait asked doubtfully.

"No, not really. Cirre got scared when Louie started reeling off the facts and figures. He tried to run. But with a little more friendly persuasion he reluctantly showed us the book. Dolph is staying with him at his apartment until you can present the findings to the board on Monday. Cirre looked like he wanted to leave town, but you might need him." He nodded toward the book in her hands. "Louie said there's enough information there to blow the lid off the entire racket."

"Enough to incriminate Campos as site supervisor?"

Dominic gauged her carefully. "Yes. That's a decision you have to make, of course."

"What do you think Miron's reaction would be?" she probed.

Dominic shrugged. "You're up against tremendous.

odds, Cait. They've never met you, yet within a week and a half of landing here, you're going to try to convince them that their site superintendent is involved in a scandal. Plus, you're a woman." He caught her angry gaze.

"Well," she snapped tersely, "they're in for some shocks, I'm afraid."

He shook his head. "You amaze me. You look so damn fragile, yet your backbone is made of steel."

Cait savored the gentle tenor of his words. At that moment, she didn't feel made of metal; rather, the longing look in his eyes made her body pliant with barely suppressed needs. Talk of work and boardrooms made her uncomfortable in the revealing robe.

"You look awfully tired yourself," she commented. "Are you all right?"

"I'm fine. But"—he glanced toward the kitchen—"starved."

She grimaced. "I know. There's no food except for some canned goods."

"How about if I take you out to eat?"

Her pulse raced, and a blush stained her cheeks. She basked in his gaze, which seemed to melt over her body, as the orange-scented breeze had earlier. It made her feel clean and refreshed.

He misread her hesitancy. "It will give me a chance to fill you in on the details. We can make it a business affair." A quick, humorless smile touched his mouth as he rose. "That way you can use it as a tax write-off."

The crystalline spell shattered between them. Irritated, Cait tucked the record book under her arm and glared at him. "Fine. I'll buy." Immediately she wanted to kick herself for overreacting. Why did she allow him to affect her so strongly?

A spark of mirth glittered in his amber eyes. "No, this time I'll buy," he said, brooking no argument.

Just as quickly as it had come, Cait felt the anger between them dissipate. She managed a small smile. "A male chauvinist after all?" she commented.

A corner of his mouth quirked at her jibe. "It was my invitation, señora. Next time you can ask me. Fair enough?"

"Fair enough."

On the way to the restaurant, she stole a quick glance at Dominic, who was resting his head against the back seat of the taxi, his eyes shut. Gone was the mask that kept his true feelings so effectively hidden. Instead there was vulnerability in his mouth, and an almost boyish cast to his face. A ribbon of care invaded Cait's heart.

As the taxi pulled to a stop in front of the Jockey Club, Dominic awakened, as if on cue. Cait's heart took an erratic leap as he turned and smiled at her sleepily.

"You nose-dive too," she said.

Rubbing his face tiredly, he paid the cabbie. "Force of habit. Ready to eat?" He held his hand out for her. Cait placed her fingers within his firm grasp and found herself standing only inches from him.

Dominic smiled lazily and slipped her arm beneath his own as they sauntered toward the brightly lit entrance.

The doorman's tobacco-brown face lit up with unabashed pleasure when he saw Dominic. He saluted smartly as they entered. Inside, sleek-looking women circulated through the rustic interior. Cait clenched her purse as almond-eyed beauties appraised Dominic with more than passing interest. She felt heat rushing into her face.

They left the main dining room behind as the maître d' led them down a rich mahogany corridor bathed with flickering lamplight. At the second door he bowed them into a miniature dining room, complete with their own waiter, who seated them. Menus appeared as if by magic, and Cait swallowed hard. She looked up to see Dominic's amused expression.

"I thought we were just going out to grab a bite to eat."

"You don't approve, señora?"

She noted the teasing in his voice and relaxed. "Yes, it's very...elegant. Private."

"If I may, I'd like to order for us."

"Certainly, it's your territory."

He grinned, instructed the attentive waiter, then added, "Not exactly a fast-food restaurant, is it?"

"No. You must be a member in good standing, to deserve a private room."

He gave her an enigmatic smile and poured a bright-red wine into her crystal glass. "The mood I'm in right now, plus a lack of sleep, makes this a more comfortable place for me."

"That makes two of us," she agreed.

He raised his glass in a toast. "Here's to better times. For both of us." They clinked glasses gently.

She sipped the ruby liquid, never breaking contact with his curiously golden eyes. "An excellent burgundy," she murmured, her fingers caressing the stem of the glass.

"From Mendoza. They're harvesting grapes up there right now. It makes for a lot of fun, dancing and just generally a relaxed atmosphere."

"Not like the site."

"No. Nothing like our site."

The waiter brought their salad quickly, then withdrew.

"What do you do for pleasure?" Dominic asked, his voice breaking into her thoughts. Cait glanced up.

"I ride horses when I'm home, do a little trout fishing."

"No needlepoint or knitting?"

Her eyes danced with mirth. "And no crocheting or quilt blocking. Now, does that fill the gamut of my womanly duties you were curious about?"

Dominic maintained an even expression, but she saw crinkles at the corners of his eyes. "As my father would say, you are *más allá de la tradición.* Beyond tradition."

"Is that a Spanish way of saying I'm a women's libber?"

Dominic shrugged, leaned back and savored another mouthful of wine, regarding her through half-closed eyes. "Not necessarily. Even in Argentina some of the old, rigid customs are finally beginning to ease."

She toyed with her glass. "And how do you feel about women's expanded role?"

"I think it's provocative . . ."

The conversation was getting too intimate for Cait, and she squirmed. The silence between them deepened.

The waiter brought a medium-rare steak sprinkled with large mushrooms and basted in butter. Hungrily Cait sliced off a succulent chunk and savored the morsel.

"I know you're being paid to turn this project

around, but this investigation could cost you your job, too," Dominic murmured.

"It's a chance I'm willing to take." She grinned. "Besides, what else am I going to do with the rest of my life?"

"The women I know unsheath their claws at high tea. I've never seen one do it at a board meeting! It ought to prove interesting."

Cait wanted to say, I'm not most women, but allowed the comment to pass. He knew she would not use her feminine wiles to get what she wanted. No, as Dave had always told her, she must go out front and attack after all the facts were in. She mustn't be afraid to put her beliefs on the line.

"Well, don't be too amused. Your job is certainly in jeopardy also."

"I knew that all along. Actually, before you came I was counting the days until they gave me my walking papers." He smiled. "You've given me a reprieve."

"Deserved, I might add. Although," Cait added, "you have to admit you didn't exactly endear yourself to anyone."

"I couldn't. For three months I took it broadside from every management super there. I was jumpy and defensive. When I finally figured out I was going to be a scapegoat, I wanted to find out why. I kept writing reports to Parker that didn't get answered. Eventually I said to hell with it and decided to make my last stand on the bridge-building phase. They might blame me, but I wasn't going to allow it to interfere with the work."

Dominic sighed deeply. "When you first came, I was enraged. I never thought you could handle a project of this size and complexity." He laughed softly and held her gaze. "I was wrong. Thank God I was wrong."

She colored fiercely and toyed nervously with the linen napkin in her lap. "Well—" she laughed lightly, "I didn't think much more of you, Dominic. You were unbelievably bad-tempered, growling and snarling at every turn. And in the print shack . . ."

"I came back that night and apologized," he defended himself.

Her voice softened as she studied his rugged features. "I know. And that's when I began to change my mind about you."

"And now, Cait?"

She swallowed with difficulty, her pulse pounding. What did he mean to her? Her mind sped over phrases and adjectives, but her heart was speaking a different language. She loved Dominic Tobbar! The realization struck her like a thunderbolt, draining the blood from her face, making her hands tremble.

She couldn't meet his eyes. She couldn't admit the overwhelming truth. "I value you as a friend, Dominic," she murmured shakily, "and I couldn't ask for a more staunch ally."

There was an awful silence. When she finally dared to glance at him, she was dumfounded by the furious black scowl on his face. His features had settled into a hard mask once again, and she felt utterly bereft.

The phone was ringing when they returned to Cait's apartment. She hurried to answer it, at the same time motioning for Dominic to come in.

"Chuck! What a surprise!" she cried into the receiver.

"I just wanted to check in with you," Chuck replied

at the other end. "I read your last report, and it sounds pretty disturbing. What's going on down there?"

She sat down on the sofa, pushing her dark hair over her shoulder. "Plenty." She rapidly filled him in on the details, aware some ten minutes later of Dominic pouring two snifters of brandy. She held out her hand to receive the glass, nodding her thanks.

"Okay, okay..." Chuck Goodell finally agreed, "I'll be on the first flight possible. You do realize the implications of all this, Cait? If you don't win your case, this could result in a horrendous law suit between the two corporations."

Cait sighed, taking a sip of the apricot brandy. "I'm aware of all the ramifications, Chuck. Now, please, pack your very best three-piece suit and get down here."

"I'll let you know when I arrive."

She replaced the receiver and began pacing the length of the living room. Outside, the lights of BA danced in the darkness like a diamond necklace. She stopped, shaking her head. "Out there... it looks so peaceful."

Dominic joined her, his shoulder inches from her own. "You handled yourself well."

She glanced up, a tight smile on her mouth. "Thanks. It's bad enough when the stakes are high, but to be a single woman in the midst of a bunch of male lions..."

"Take it easy," he soothed. "You'll do fine." He set the snifter on the coffee table, a self-deprecating grin on his face. "If you can keep me in line, you can make the chairman of the board jump through hoops."

She laughed with him and turned, accompanying

him to the door. "Only because you allowed me to put you into line, Dominic." She paused, finding the next words difficult to say. "Dominic," she finally whispered, "you asked me before what I think of you now. You know you're more than *just* a friend." Her eyes pleaded with him to understand.

He nodded and raised her cool hand to his lips. *"Buenas noches, mi leona,"* he murmured.

A quiver of delight sprang through her, and Cait's lips parted as he raised his head, still holding her fingers. His amber eyes studied her, and her breath snagged, her heart leaping with unbidden excitement as she swayed forward. The masculine scent of his body was like a perfume to her spinning senses. She was only partly aware that he had pulled her closer, her head tilted, ready to meet his strong, generous mouth.

The warmth of his breath fanned across her face. His mouth, moving slowly across her lips, parted them. The pressure became insistent, a powerful intoxicant. A soft noise vibrated from her throat as he crushed her against his hard, muscular body, his mouth bruising her own in a breath-stealing kiss. Dazed by the barely suppressed passion quivering within his tightly checked body, Cait suddenly found herself at arm's length from him. Her lips throbbed from the bruising force, and she unconsciously raised her fingertips to them, staring wide-eyed.

He frowned. "I'm sorry," he murmured huskily. "I got a little carried away..."

"That's—it's all right," she reassured him, her voice throaty and faraway. Dave had never kissed her like that! A tinge of guilt washed over her, and she blushed fiercely, pulling out of his grasp and standing uncertainly in front of him.

He shook his head, as if displeased with himself. "No, I can see it's not at all right," he growled. "It would be easy if you were like all the rest. But you aren't. I don't want to frighten you away."

She breathed deeply, the remnants of the kiss still sparking the embers of her own hungering thirst for physical contact. "You've never scared me, Dominic . . . not ever. It's just that I don't get kissed like that every day." She managed a small smile that seemed to soothe him.

"Sure?"

"Positive . . . very positive." She wanted to say, "Never stop," but she remained silent.

"How about breakfast tomorrow morning?" he murmured.

The power of the spell he had woven moments before still lingered, and she felt herself falling back into its warm embrace. "Breakfast?" Who was hungry? Right now all she could be aware of was her thudding heart. "Uh—what time?"

A tender smile played on his mouth, as if he enjoyed her distraction. "Nine?"

"Sure. Where will you be staying? I mean—isn't it too late to book a reservation at a hotel?"

He picked up his bag. "There's an apartment I stay at when I'm in BA. In case you need to get hold of me, write down this phone number."

Cait scratched it down and then watched him open the door to leave. "Wait," she called.

He turned. "Yes?"

"My Spanish is rusty. What did you call me just a few minutes ago?"

He smiled. "My Lioness. I'll see you tomorrow morning."

She stood staring at the ivory door after he left. The room suddenly felt barren without his vibrant presence, and she sank slowly onto the couch. He had called her his lioness.

But just before she fell asleep, the scent of ripe oranges wafting through the open window, a treacherous thought made her eyes fly open. *Whose* apartment was Dominic staying in? He hadn't said it was *his* apartment. She chided herself for being silly, but a growing suspicion wouldn't go away.

Chapter Eight

WHEN THE KNOCK CAME, Cait's heart leaped in response. Dominic smiled genially in the doorway, looking fresh and boyishly youthful in a dark navy-blue shirt and white slacks. The darkness of his tan made him look even more handsome, and she found herself smiling in return.

"It's a beautiful morning," he said, holding out his hand.

Unconsciously she placed her fingers within his and nodded, feeling a blush sweep her cheeks. They hurried down the stairs and past the doorman, who bowed with a grin and a flourish of his cap. Stepping out into the crisp morning air, Cait breathed in deeply, her eyes wide with excitement.

"I feel like a kid," she breathed.

Dominic agreed as he opened the door of the silver Porsche parked alongside the curb. "You look like a child on Christmas."

Cait relaxed in the front seat. The roar of the sports car reminded her of a deep growl of a cat. "Is this your car?" she asked.

He nodded, smoothly shifting gears. "Does it fit your image of me?" She saw the glitter of humor in his eyes.

"What gave you the idea I had an image of you?"

"I made a poor impression the first night we met. I hope I'm changing what you thought of me then."

Cait tore her gaze from his rugged profile, wanting to stare at him for hours to study that mobile face, which seemed to change like the tide. "I learned a long time ago not to overrate first impressions. I always give everyone plenty of rope to hang himself on."

He grinned, turning the corner and driving down a larger avenida studded with flowers and palms. "If I'd been a cat, I would have used up eight of my nine lives with you."

Cait laughed with him. "You are a cat," she returned. "A jaguar." She didn't bother to explain what she meant, and he didn't ask. She felt wonderfully happy and alive.

The streets were quiet as they sped by. Women with fine lace shawls over their heads were walking to church, followed by their children, immaculately clean in blue-and-white uniforms, and their husbands, dressed in formal suits and hats. Peacefulness seemed to envelop the cosmopolitan city as they drove through the heart of BA. Eventually Dominic pointed to an expensive-looking restaurant.

"La Cautiva. I thought you might enjoy a North American breakfast of eggs and bacon instead of *desayuno*."

"You're right. I am a big fan of breakfast. But what is desayuno?"

"Desayuno is the Argentine version of breakfast," Dominic explained as they got out of the car. "It consists of coffee, a roll and perhaps some jam or honey." He smiled, glancing down at her. "But you need a few big breakfasts to put some meat on those bones."

Cait wrinkled her nose and stepped into the dimly lit interior. "Not you too! I suppose Louie has been prompting you."

Dominic only smiled. Cait sat down across from him in a black leather booth and studied the menu, which was written in Spanish.

"I'm in trouble," she muttered, peeking up over the top.

"You? Never."

She grinned. "Superwoman I'm not. Would you like to point out the eggs and bacon?"

"Don't worry, I'll order them for you." A waiter seemed to appear from nowhere. She enjoyed the purring baritone of Dominic's voice as he ordered their meal.

"And what if I had been Superwoman?" she asked, picking up their previous conversation after their coffee had been poured.

"I certainly would not have invited your temper." He laughed. "You are más allá de la tradición. I can deal with that."

She placed her elbows on the table, letting her dark hair frame her face. "My father did not raise me on dolls and tea parties, you know."

He sobered slightly. "He must be a very special person to have allowed you to be yourself. Never liked dolls?"

She shook her head, a smile edging her full mouth. "No. I can't ask the same of you. You're obviously in a very male occupation."

He shrugged, a thread of what Cait interpreted as pain in his eyes. "Not so obviously. As I told you, my father wanted me to be a physician."

"Somehow I don't picture you as a doctor, Dominic. There's—" she groped for the correct words, "a freedom about you that demands to be outdoors." She shrugged, smiling shyly. "A jaguar needs the freedom of his territory. I don't think an operating room would give it to you."

He stared at her hard. "You continually surprise me with your understanding." A shiver ran down her spine at his warm gaze, and her cheeks grew flushed. "Tell me," he said, "did you always want to be an engineer?"

She laughed to mask her confusion. "Just about. My father was an architect, and from the time I was seven, I went with him to the office. He explained what he was doing, and I guess it just rubbed off." Her eyes came alive with excitement, and her voice grew hushed. "But most of all, I loved the times he took me out to the construction sites. The loud roar of those huge trucks and the activity of strong men molding steel into beauty...well, you understand that...you build bridges."

"Yes, I do understand that. And love it...as you do." He shook his head. "I have the damndest time believing a woman could feel as I do about construc-tion. Down here, in Argentina, to tell you the truth, I don't think there is a single woman engineer in the whole country." He toyed with the ornate silver spoon, frowning. Cait sensed that he was deep in thought.

After breakfast they drove to the Plaza de Mayo, in the center of BA, and strolled toward the circular pool. Dominic still seemed far away.

"Dominic . . . ?" Cait began hesitantly. He looked down at her, a tender flame in his golden gaze. She swallowed and plunged ahead with her half-formed thought. "There must have been a great deal of pain over your decision to become an engineer instead of a surgeon. Has your father finally accepted your career?"

She sensed his nerves jangle rawly at such a personal question. His brow furrowed and his lips thinned as he halted, throwing his hands on his hips. It was a gesture he made whenever he was upset but trying to effectively deal with a situation. She cringed.

"My father is a man of tradition, Cait. He could not understand my decision, tolerate it or"—he sighed—"forgive it."

"But he must have forgiven you!"

He smiled absently. "Let's put it this way. I've been a disappointment to my father in many ways."

He took her hand. "This is Casa Rosada, the pink house," he said, changing the subject. "Perhaps you might think of Plaza de Mayo as a general meeting place. The Peróns stood on that balcony, and thousands crowded into this plaza to hear them. Old men come here in the mornings to warm their backs in the sun. The pigeons come, because they know the old men will feed them. Look, there's a group of children just arriving from church. Let's sit down and watch them for a moment."

Cait sat quietly, aware of their bodies meeting at

arm and thigh. She looked at the way he held his head. He was a man of immense pride and self-assurance.

"Did I tell you how lovely you look in a dress?"

She turned, lips parted in surpise. His voice had stolen into her thoughts like a welcome breeze. She smiled simply. "Thank you. You probably thought I was born in blue jeans, right?"

Dominic returned her smile. "There is such a blinding difference to you, like day and night, Cait Monahan." His voice caressed her, and she trembled. "You continually amaze me. How many sides of you are there?" His thumb traveled the length of her jaw, trailing down the side of her slender neck. Her pulse leaped crazily, and she felt his fingers slide behind her neck and pull her toward him. Automatically she closed her eyes, her lips yielding as his mouth lightly touched her own. A flame leaped to life within her, and she gave in to the pressure of his arm, her body swaying against his hard chest. A moan of pleasure rose in her throat as his tongue forced entry into her mouth, and her breath was suspended as a vortex of fire uncoiled within her quivering body.

He dragged his mouth from her lips, his eyes burning with a fierce light of desire. Cait lost herself in his hypnotic gaze, her heart pounding without relief in her aching breast. She was trembling and felt weakened by the sudden kiss. It had been so unexpected, so devasting, that her green eyes were flecked with the gold of awakening desire. She saw confusion in his gaze as he drank in her upturned face. He released her slowly. "Who are you? What are you doing to me?" he demanded rawly.

Cait was stunned by the accusation in his voice. It took her precious moments to recover, to pull herself out of that magnetic vortex that had held her a willing captive. "Do you think I'm doing something I'm not supposed to?" she asked, stung. "Are women in blue jeans not supposed to react to a kiss the way other women do?"

"I haven't decided what motivates you," he returned slowly, still appraising her. "You're like a heady wine. You make me feel irresponsible and reckless." A self-deprecating smile cut across his mouth. "I'm too old to behave like an eighteen-year-old boy again."

Cait wasn't sure whether she should feel insulted or complimented. She colored fiercely, embarrassed at how easily he had pulled down her defenses and gently nudged embers of desire into life. Getting to her feet, she said, "I can assure you I'm not a siren who has cast a spell on you."

He rose easily, walking at her side. "Positive?"

She relaxed, hearing the edge of humor in his voice again. Maybe he had not planned that kiss. Maybe it had just happened and caught them both off guard. "Very positive."

Dominic laid a hand on her shoulder, gently pulling her to a stop and forcing her to turn and face him. "I'm not sorry it happened, Cait, just puzzled as to why I can't get enough of you."

Her anger soared once again, and her green eyes darkened. "Thanks a lot!"

He laughed richly. "You misunderstand, querida. I simply can't resist your attractions. Apology accepted?"

She had pulled away, her hands on her hips in an imperious gesture. "I would hate to go around pre-planning every damn move I made!"

One black eyebrow rose, and his eyes danced with mirth. "Ah . . . you like to live dangerously, is that it? Spontaneity in place of caution?"

She colored more fiercely, feeling at odds with him. "No, I don't throw caution to the winds either. But you seem to want to put me conveniently in some box or under some label, and I refuse to fit your idea of how a woman is supposed to act."

He slipped his hand beneath her elbow, and they began to walk at a slower, more relaxed pace. "As I said before, the only kind of women I know unsheath their claws at high tea. Can I help it if you walk into my life and contradict everything I thought I knew about women?"

She gave him a sidelong glance. "At your age, Dominic, you have either cheated yourself out of knowing many different kinds of women or you were very badly hurt by someone." Cait gulped hard, watching his reaction to her hotly flung words. She hadn't meant to hurt him. She felt his fingers tighten momentarily, and she muttered, "Oh, forget what I said. It's your fault, you know. When I get angry, I don't stop and think before I speak. I'm sorry."

He leaned down and opened the door to the Porsche, a careless smile on his lips. "Your Irish comes out at the most interesting times, Cait. Climb in; I'm going to take you someplace to cool down."

As they sped through the avenidas, the Rio de la Plata came into view. Beautifully sculpted buildings of beige, sandstone and marble gave way to long, rectangular wooden and aluminum structures that dotted the wharf area. Dominic parked along Cangallo and switched off the engine, leaning back and surveying her through dark lashes.

"All right, my brave lioness, are you ready to explore La Boca?" He smiled. "Or should I rephrase that and ask if La Boca is ready for you?"

She was. The odors of the dock assailed her as she walked to the front of the car. Salt air was mixed with the smell of the blue-green river. Seagulls wheeled and flapped around the cranes, docked ships and huge housing sheds that held the unloaded cargos.

Dominic took her hand to guide her, explaining that ships came in from around the world to transport Argentine beef, hides and tallow. She watched with interest as beef hides, stacked fifty to seventy-five per pallet, were lifted by cable onto a waiting Japanese ship.

The colorful dress of the longshoremen, and of the women who lingered against the stolid brown walls of the sheds, reminded Cait of tropical birds. Tantalizing scents wafted in on the early afternoon air.

"What is that delicious smell?" she asked.

Dominic sniffed and smiled. "Are you hungry again?"

She grinned. "It must be the salt air."

"Come on, I'll show you exactly where it's coming from."

They turned a corner that led away from the dock area, and Cait found herself weaving in and out of narrow alleys littered with trash. "Is this place safe at night?" she asked.

"A long time ago La Boca had a nasty reputation

for hot-blooded arguments between gauchos over their kept women and betting. Nowadays it isn't wise for women to travel these back streets alone, even though La Boca has changed drastically since that time."

Cait enjoyed the bright reds, yellows and blues of the houses they now passed. She glanced at Dominic. He seemed so boyish now, so unlike the rugged, stubborn, defensive engineer from the site. She recognized a change in herself as well. No longer did she try to throw up her supervisory façade and remain cool and detached. Dominic made her feel free to be herself.

They climbed the creaking wooden steps of a red house garishly painted with green trim, and entered a dimly lit foyer. Cait's grip on Dominic's hand tightened as her eyes adjusted to the gloom. He hailed the waiter, who shrugged his shoulders eloquently.

"Any seat in the house, señor. What's your choice?"

Dominic chose a corner table and ordered their food, then rested his elbows on the table, smiling at her.

"And what is so funny?" she asked.

"Nothing. I'm just happy. How about you?"

The words had been spoken softly, a caress, and Cait held his amber gaze. "Yes ... I am too ..."

With a flourish, their waiter returned with the first course. Small golden fish lay on a ceramic plate heavily granished with parsley.

"Pescaditos," Dominic explained, putting half of the fare on her plate. "They're little fish that are fried until crisp, and are considered a delicacy of La Boca. Go ahead, try one," he urged.

She cautiously tasted one small fish. "Mmm, they're delicious," she exclaimed.

The waiter brought the next course, a heaping bowl of ravioli, smelling of tomato and oregano. Cait dished Dominic a healthy serving.

"Would you like some music?" he asked.

"Sure. Where's the orchestra?"

He nodded toward the waiter, who walked up on a small stage. "Him. If you love opera, you'll love La Boca. Listen." To her surprise, the waiter broke into an operatic tenor.

The autumn sun was stong when they emerged from the restaurant sometime later. Cait's laughter bubbled as she nimbly descended the stairs, turning to meet Dominic. He smiled and slid his arm about her shoulders, pulling her close to him as they strolled in companionable silence.

Cait sighed with contentment. "I think the wine got to me. That isn't any ten percent alcohol content in that wine, is it?"

"No. Now you can see why sailors and gauchos used to fly into a rage after drinking a bottle. Do you know that the tango actually originated in this district?"

"That was one of the few things I knew about Argentina," she admitted. "Cattle, the tango and gauchos.

He nodded and gave her a brief hug. "My father owns an *estancia* and runs about five thousand head of cattle on the land plus a hundred thoroughbreds for racing."

Cait raised her brows in amazement. "Doctoring

must be financially rewarding down here."

"The estancia has been in the family since the sixteen hundreds, Cait. It's a custom," he put in drily, "that the first-born son gets a proper education in a proper field and then practices being a professional as well as a rich land baron."

"And you didn't want either title?" she hedged.

"No, never. I love the land, but in a different way than my father."

She smiled. "So what else is expected of a rich son of an estancia owner?"

"The usual," he replied. "Attending social fetes, the Colon opera opening, running for public office, a beautiful wife and many children..."

"I see," she murmured. They came to a halt at the silver Porsche, and Cait waited for him to unlock her door. "So none of it rubbed off on you?"

Dominic smiled grimly, helping her in. "Some of it did, and it proved to be a disaster." Cait wondered at his tight-lipped reply but refrained from asking. The interior of the car was heated by the sun's rays and made her feel drowsy. She laid her head back. A languorous smile played on her lips, and she barely opened her eyes.

"I had a wonderful time, Dominic. Thank you. And I'm glad you shed that estancia image. La Boca is far more exciting than the very best restaurant in BA."

He relaxed against the seat, resting his hand on the steering wheel. "There is something about this district that weaves a spell over people who come here. I'm happy you enjoyed it. It felt good to laugh again." There was a wistful tone in his voice.

Cait sat up, studying his relaxed features. Her instincts warned her not to ask the obvious question about the "disaster" that seemed to hover around him. They were still learning to trust each other. He would tell her someday. But in the meantime she couldn't help but wonder.

Chapter Nine

CHUCK GOODELL, a man of wiry build and intense blue eyes, arrived at Cait's apartment the next morning. He met Cait and Louie with a serious handshake and nod of his head.

Louie motioned the vice-president to sit down on the sofa. "You look a little peaked, Chuck," he jibed.

"I am," Chuck growled. Cait joined him, pushing back some papers and handing him the record book. "Thanks to Dominic and Louie, we have the proof we need to present to the Miron officials."

"Who's Dominic?"

"Bridge superintendent," Louie volunteered. "Damn fine one, judging from how well he's done with the little support he's been given."

"I see." Goodell's brows drew together in a V of concentration as Cait began to explain the figures. Within two hours, she saw his face sag from the grim reality of it. Finally around six o'clock, Goodell slapped the book shut and stood up. He rubbed the back of his neck tiredly and glanced down at Cait.

"I put you in a hell of a position, didn't I?"

She nodded, also standing. "It gets worse. Dominic seems to think that the board chairman will shove me out of the room, because I'm más allá de la tradición." She explained the terminology.

"Where is this Dominic Tobbar fellow?" Chuck asked.

"Here in BA," Louie mentioned, getting up and refilling his coffee cup. "You want to see him?"

"Yes, I think it best. Cait, can you get him over here this evening?"

"I'll call and find out. Hold on." She went to the bedroom to make the call. A sultry voice answered. Cait's fingers tightened on the receiver.

"I'm trying to get hold of Señor Dominic Tobbar. Is he there, please?"

There was silence at the other end, and Cait felt her heart wrench in pain. "Sí. May I ask who is calling?"

"Cait Monahan."

"One moment . . ."

Cait thought she heard the rustle of silk and she compressed her lips. Who was this woman? A mistress? Dominic never had said where he was staying. . . . More pain filled her heart, and she suddenly felt betrayed. Anger flooded through her, and when he answered, her voice was more than slightly clipped.

"Chuck Goodell wants to see you this evening. Do you think you can get over here?"

"Of course. I'll be right there, Cait."

She wrestled with the tumult of despair, anger and jealousy that the phone call had ignited. But when Dominic arrived, she managed a tight smile of greeting. He gave her a searching look before moving to where Goodell stood, but he said nothing.

The foursome sat down in the living room, and Cait had to force herself to focus on the conversation. Occasionally she felt Dominic's questioning gaze upon her. Once their eyes met, and she glared at him across the coffee table, feeling the heat of her anger very close to surfacing.

Louie got up an hour later, groaning and rubbing his back. "I don't know about the rest of you, but I'm going back to my hotel to sleep. How about you, Chuck?"

"I'll come too." He rose and looked at Cait, a grim expression on his face. "Well, Cait, I think this about does it."

She agreed. "Got your three-piece suit?"

"Yep. Just like you said." He extended his hand to Dominic. "Thanks for your help. It's been invaluable in piecing this messy problem together."

Dominic returned the handshake. "I can't think of anyone better than Cait to present this case, and I know she's glad you came. So am I."

Cait felt panic rising in her throat as her two friends trailed out. Dominic rose to his full height, his hands draped loosely on his hips, scrutinizing her. Swallowing hard, she turned and met his gaze directly.

"Something's wrong," he prodded.

"Whatever gave you that idea?" She wasn't a very good liar, and cringed at the high pitch of her voice. Unable to remain under his gaze, she picked up the used coffee cups and walked into the kitchen to rinse them out. He followed, leaning against the counter only a few inches from where she stood.

"You don't hide your anger well, Cait. Why are

you upset? Was it something I did, or does it have to do with that meeting tomorrow?"

"I'm not angry!" There, she'd done it. Damn her Irish temper.

A grudging smile edged his mouth. "Your claws are showing, querida."

Cait turned, her eyes blazing with barely controlled anger. "Look, I'm tired and I'm tense. All right? Just call it a night, Dominic..."

"Not yet," he murmured. "I care enough for you to want to listen to what has made you angry."

"I suppose you tell that to every woman you meet," she returned sarcastically, stalking out of the kitchen and sitting down on the couch. He leaned casually against the kitchen entrance, his arms folded against his chest, watching her.

"No, I don't go around pretending to care when I don't."

Her nostrils flared with contempt. "I was married a long time, Dominic, and I don't know how to play the silly games single men and women play. But I'm learning...damn, I'm learning the hard way."

His eyes darkened. He walked into the living room and knelt down beside her. "What games?" he probed. "Will you please tell me what this is all about?"

She started to rise; he was too close. But his hand shot out, gripping her arm.

"Cait," he growled, "stand still for two seconds and tell me what's making you so damned irritable."

"You!" she snapped, pulling free of his grip. She rubbed her arm where he had touched it. "I should have known better..." she stumbled on, "that you'd have a mistress. I should have believed all those silly tales about men having three or four mistresses here and there—"

He threw back his head and laughed deeply, his voice carrying throughout the apartment. Cait blushed crimson and leaped away from him, standing by the balcony doors. Her dark hair lay in disarray about her proud shoulders, and she lifted her chin defiantly as he came to her side. A tender smile remained on his mouth, and he reached out, taming one of those rebellious tresses.

"Mi leona," he murmured, "the woman who answered the phone was my sister, Lucianna."

Her gaze dropped. "Oh . . ."

"Green eyes . . . you know, I didn't take you for being the jealous sort."

"I'm not usually! So stop smirking like the cat that just ate the canary." She stepped away, supressing a desire to simply run away from him. He sat next to her, his hands resting against his thighs.

"So you thought I had a mistress?"

"Yes," she answered stubbornly, refusing to meet his eyes. "I don't believe in affairs outside of marriage. I don't care how antiquated that sounds. I had a good marriage, Dominic, and I would never think of getting involved with a man who was married or involved with other women."

He eyed her thoughtfully. "Yes, I can see that now. For a woman who is más allá de la tradición, you have the morals of my parents' generation."

"And don't you?" she flung at him angrily, her eyes glittering with emerald fire.

"Let's just say I agree with you in principal, Cait. I was forced into an arranged marriage with a woman who, I found out sometime later, had no morals." A twisted smile came to his mouth. "Or, let's say, very few."

The anger drained out of Cait in a blinding instant. She sat staring at the naked pain evident in his expression.

"I see," she murmured. She heaved a long sigh and planted her chin in the palms of her hands, staring down at the tiled floor. "We're so different," she said quietly. "I came from such a fantastic marriage, and yours was less than good. I often wonder if any relationship can ever equal what I had before, and I'm sure you look at every woman and her potential to cheat on you again." She gave a humorless laugh. "What a pair we are, huh?"

The silence deepened, and she finally looked up at Dominic. "I'd like to know where you got your insight," he said, and then shook his head, getting to his feet. He towered above her, and she felt suddenly very lonely and isolated from him.

"Life gave it to me, Dominic. Hasn't it taught you to be perceptive too?" she challenged softly, holding his gaze.

"All I see are manipulators." He shrugged. "We're all puppets to someone or something; it's inevitable."

"And you don't manipulate?"

That bitter, cutting smile came to his mouth. "Yes, one must do it to survive."

"Your ex-wife must have had more than claws," she murmured, "to have made you so wary of everyone's gestures toward you. No wonder you were so defensive at the site with me at first..." Her voice trailed off into the mellowing silence. "There is trust, you know. Not everyone is going to knife you in the back or play you for a fool. Haven't I proven that at the site? How can you think that I'm manipulating you for my own gain?"

He reached out, his hand sliding over the crown of her head, following the silken curve of her hair. "You've proven your mettle so far, Cait Monahan, and you've made me stop to evaluate what I thought was a generalization for every woman I've ever known." His voice became husky. "But you . . . Dios, you break every rule. There is a freedom about you, mi leona, that sometimes frightens me." A sad smile remained on his mouth. "And at the same time, I am mesmerized by your actions and your logic. The only feminine logic I've seen is catty and double-edged. You speak your mind and line it with tact, which I find refreshing." He rested his hand against her shoulder, his fingers brushing her strong jaw. "That's why, earlier today, I asked what you were . . ."

A lump of hurt formed in her throat, and it was painful to swallow. She felt tears stinging her eyes and was angry with herself. He *would* interpret her tears as pity for him, and for some reason Cait didn't want him to misread those tears of compassion. Hesitantly she raised her hand, touching his cheek, finding his skin warm and inviting. "You see what I am," she whispered.

He uttered a low groan, pulling her into his arms in a fierce, crushing embrace. Her body flattened willingly against his chest and hips, her arms encircling his thickly corded neck.

"Oh . . . Dominic," she sighed close to his ear.

She felt his mouth linger tantalizingly on her throat,

leaving a fiery brand of kisses, moving slowly toward the open collar of her dress. His strong, vital hands roved across her back and down to encompass her rounded hips, pulling her savagely against him in urgency. She gasped, feeling his insistent maleness pressing against her.

"I want you . . ." he breathed hoarsely, nibbling at her ear. He pushed her roughly away, his nostrils flared, his breathing coming in heavy gasps. "Soon . . ." His voice was gravelly with passion, vibrating through Cait's straining, begging senses. "Very soon," he gulped, and then managed a grimace. He ran his hands along her arms in a more gentle fashion. "Believe me, if this business problem weren't around, things would be different tonight," he promised.

After he left, Cait trembled and wrapped her arms about her body as she stood alone in the enveloping silence.

"Good morning. Did you sleep well?" said a familiar voice over the telephone.

Cait snuggled against the pillows, drowsily opening her eyes. "Yes." She smiled wistfully, the timbre of Dominic's voice acting like a gentle hand pulling her slowly into wakefulness.

"No nightmares?"

"No, just nice dreams . . ."

"It's about time. Listen, I called you for several reasons. Are you awake enough to think?" The humorous tinge in his voice made her smile again, and she struggled to sit up in bed, her hair falling about her shoulders.

"Yes, go ahead."

"First, I'm going over to Cirre's apartment to stay there with Dolph and his men. If they corner you in that meeting and want Cirre, give me a call and we'll produce him for you. I don't think it's wise to leave our storekeeper unattended right now."

She rubbed her eyes. "Do you think Campos knows we have the book?"

"I don't know . . . you'll find out soon enough. Apparently both of them go their separate ways once they come to BA. So Campos may not even be aware of what has taken place. And—" he hesitated, "if he's caught off guard, all hell might break loose. Just make sure you use Goodell as a shield against anything he might say."

She was grateful for his concern. "I've been yelled and cursed at by better men, believe me. I weathered it in the past; I'll do the same now, although I don't enjoy it."

"It's that sadistic Irish streak coming out in you. All fire."

Cait chuckled softly. "And I suppose you're as placid as water?" She heard his rich laugher.

"One is enough, thank you," he returned, referring to Cait's volatile temper.

"Not oil and water, eh?"

"More like oil and fire. We seem to create an explosion when we're together, don't we?"

She vividly recalled their first meeting and then the episode at the print shack. . . . He had a fierce temper. "You won't get an argument out of me on that point."

"Well, listen, mi leona, I could sit here and talk with you all day long, but we both have work to do. Call me after the meeting, and I'll come down and pick you all up and we'll go eat."

For some reason, she felt as if her magic weekend was evaporating. They were going back to the site so soon, but she wanted to explore more of BA with Dominic. She sighed. "I had a wonderful weekend, Dominic."

The line grew silent, and then Cait heard that purr in his voice. "No more than I did, querida. We'll do it again."

"Promise?"

"My word of honor. Listen, be careful in that meeting."

She basked in his concern. "I'm just glad you'll be there to meet us afterward."

"You're going to win, Cait. You have truth on your side."

"Just having you believe in me is enough," she said softly, meaning it.

"Querida, I'll see you at noon."

"Wait . . . Dominic, what is that word you keep calling me—que—"

"Querida."

"What does it mean?"

"I'll reserve a special time and place to tell you that, mi leona. Buenos días, querida."

She stared at the phone for a moment, the rough tongue of his voice almost a physical touch upon her body. Smiling absently, she replaced the receiver, remaining dreamily on that cloud he had woven about her.

Chapter Ten

As THEY FILED OUT of the elevator of the Miron Corporation building in a tight knot, Cait cast a final glance over at Louie. He winked and offered her an encouraging smile. She clutched her briefcase and squared her shoulders as they turned toward the board-room located at the end of the hall.

Señor di Grazzi introduced Cait under the "new business" portion of the board meeting. "Señora Cait Monahan, Brentworth project superintendent, will now give us our first look at the delay which has been caused at the site. We feel fortunate to have such a lovely young woman in our billion-dollar joint venture with Brentworth. Please, Señora Monahan, come take the podium."

Irritation grated against her fear. His introduction sounded very much like a setup. Since when would any board chairman announce such an important topic with such obvious flattery? It was not going to be easy to make them see her as the project superintendent. Her mouth was dry, and she took a drink of water before beginning her report. She saw Campos sitting relaxed, his gaze interested, his hands clasped in front of him expectantly. He doesn't know, Cait realized, and felt a snaking coil of fear in the pit of her stomach.

She missed none of the facial expressions or the change in subtle body language as she began explaining why the project was behind schedule. She built her case carefully. When Louie Henning got up and distributed xeroxed copies of several fact sheets, she began to see faces tighten, lips taking on a firmer line. The silence in the room became deafening. Campos looked two shades lighter, his hands now clenched in a knot in front of his body.

At the mention of Cirre's name, Campos's eyes swung to Cait. She met them fearlessly. She quickly told how Dominic and Louie had weighed, measured and counted the supplies on the site and calculated that the amount lost was worth nearly six hundred thousand dollars. A collective intake of breath broke the quiet, and Cait boldly continued. Finally Louie produced a signed statement from Cirre admitting his guilt in juggling the books.

Di Grazzi was frowning heavily, his gray eyebrows thick with displeasure.

"Gentlemen," Cait continued, "a scheme of this magnitude does not occur overnight and not without significant help from the managerial and supervisory levels. We have evidence which implicates a very top Miron official at the site, and I am asking you today to relieve him of his duties and allow me to choose a replacement."

Di Grazzi held up the paper. "You're talking about Señor Cirre, of course?"

Campos's brown eyes were wide with fright as he

saw Cait's gaze settle on him. "Señor di Grazzi, I respectfully submit that not only Señor Cirre is involved, but of equal guilt is Señor Campos."

The room seemed to explode with silent disbelief. Di Grazzi looked absolutely stunned. Campos snarled an obscenity under his breath, then grabbed his copy, his face suffusing into a plum color. "No! This is lies! All lies!" he yelled, jumping to his feet. He clenched his fist at Cait. "This is only a game to make Miron the culprit for Brentworth's failings! It's all lies, and I won't stand here and take this sort of slander—"

"Señora Monahan?" Di Grazzi's voice was soft.

"Sir?"

"What proof"—he stressed the word slightly—"do you have that Señores Cirre and Campos collaborated on this supposed scheme?"

She pointed at the maroon book that Louie hoisted from her briefcase. "Señor Henning will turn over the second set of books, which was kept by Señor Cirre at his apartment. If you note, Señor Campos's initials confirm my allegations. I don't know your country's laws, so I will leave any legal actions in your corporation's able hands."

"Señor Campos, what is your response to this allegation and this document?"

In spite of his initial reaction in the boardroom, there was a long pause before he responded. "I can assure you, Señor di Grazzi, that the facts are not as they appear. This book is undoubtedly a forgery." Perspiration gleamed along his forehead, and he paused to regain his shattered composure. "Gentlemen, the seriousness of these allegations comes as a complete surprise to me. I believe it is in my best interests to refrain from further discussion until my attorney can be present. In view of my long association with the company and my wish not to hinder its activities, I respectfully submit my resignation."

"I'll accept your resignation," di Grazzi said with finality, "and I expect it to be dated yesterday. I suggest you retire from this meeting." Campos rose slowly, glared briefly at Cait and left the room. "Señora Monahan, whom would you suggest as a replacement for Señores Cirre and Campos until we can clear up this matter?"

"I would like Señor Henning to replace Señor Cirre as storekeeper. His thirty years in procurement and scheduling will help us plug other leaks and begin getting needed equipment on the site. With the board's permission, I recommend the installation of Señor Dominic Tobbar in place of Señor Campos. He was the only man on that site to buck the mounting problems by preparing written reports detailing the losses and back orders. I've found him honest and trustworthy. He has the managerial background for such a position, and until a full investigation is completed, he is the only one we know who is not part of this scandal."

Di Grazzi smiled coldly. "Very well, we will take your recommendation under advisement. If you would be so kind as to wait outside, I must consult our officers . . ."

Cait nodded. "Of course."

The entire presentation and its outcome had taken only two hours. By eleven-thirty, Cait was anxiously awaiting Dominic's arrival in the lobby. Di Grazzi had given her permission to install Henning and Tobbar, and she was elated. Louie ambled up to her, a gleam in his eyes.

"Well, Rose, you did it. Congratulations. How are you feelin'?"

"I think my knees are going to buckle."

"You'll be fine, darlin'. We'll be outa here in a minute. I guess Chuck is going to have lunch with di Grazzi, and we can go back to the site when we want."

"Good! Give me the dirt of Patagonia instead of all this damn political intrigue." She spotted Dominic as he threaded his way through the gathering crowd. As much as she wanted to simply run to his arms and be smothered by his protective, fierce embrace, she could not do it. Not in front of all the Miron personnel who milled around them in noontime traffic. Dominic's gaze was worried. He stopped, catching her hand briefly in his own and then letting it go.

"You look pale," he commented, frowning.

She wearily brushed aside a tendril of hair from her cheek. "We won. But at what a price! I never want to have to do it again."

"We've won round one, son," Louie corrected. "The next thing will be to take depositions, and there'll be a grand jury investigation."

Dominic glanced around, his mouth set in a grim line, his gaze worriedly assessing Cait's condition. "Let's get out of here. You need some place to relax. Anyone hungry?"

"Starved!" Cait admitted, realizing she was famished.

"What do you have in mind?" Louie asked.

"How about a good Argentine steak in celebration, and you can fill me in on the details of the battle?"

"Sounds good. Lead the way. Rose, you coming or are you rooted to the spot?"

Cait laughed nervously, feeling suddenly shaky. Dominic seemed to sense her uneasiness and looped his arm through hers, pulling her against his body. She looked up at him, nodding her thanks.

After the main course she finally broke the news about his new position. Lifting her crystal goblet toward him, she murmured, "Congratulations, Dominic. You are now the site superintendent for Miron."

Louie lifted his glass, watching the engineer's stunned expression. "Drink up, son. You've earned it."

Dominic touched their glasses. "You really are a masochist, Señora Monahan."

Cait grinned, sipping the wine with pleasure. "How's that, Señor Tobbar?"

"Do you think you can stand working elbow to elbow with me every day?"

"I think I'll force myself, for the betterment of the organization," she answered drily.

Dominic winked over at Louie. "We have another Joan of Arc on our hands."

Later, as the drone of the Beechcraft lulled Cait to the brink of sleep, Dominic asked, "Why didn't you tell me you were considering me for site superintendent?"

She turned, watching Louie snoozing peacefully in the back seat. Her gaze drifted to the engineer. "I couldn't be sure di Grazzi would let me have my way. And"—she managed a sour grin—"I couldn't be sure you would take it, either."

He pressed his lips together. "It's going to be

tough, juggling office work against the bridge portion, but I'll do it. You realize I've turned down this type of position on other job sites?"

Her eyebrows raised slightly. It was true. Twelve years in the field easily qualified him for higher managerial posts. But many engineers hated being a desk jockey and chose a field position and less pay just to remain outdoors. "No, I hadn't realized," she answered tentatively. "Then why——"

"We work well together. Despite our obvious differences."

Cait laughed. "We aren't so different, Dominic. As a matter of fact, we're very much alike in many ways."

"Such as?" A droll smile touched his mouth.

"We're both opinionated——"

"Stubborn."

"Yes, well, we're hard-working——"

"Only because we don't know any better."

"Dominic!"

"Okay, I'm teasing you. Yes, we are similar. One thing, though. Let's make a rule not to work ourselves into the ground. I don't know about you, but after all the hell I've gone through these last six months, I need some down time."

Cait agreed. "I promised to take you back into BA," Dominic continued, "and I intend to do it. Plus, I want you to see the real Argentina." He motioned northward. "The Camp, the tropical paradise of Gran Chaco, the falls . . . There's so much you must experience about this country."

Her heart leaped in response to the excitement that edged his voice. She couldn't quite believe her ears.

He wanted to spend more time with her. At first, the idea was pleasant, and then old, familiar fears began to crumble her expectations.

"Next week, come hell or high water, I'm taking Saturday and Sunday off." He reached over, his strong fingers covering her hand. "And I want you to come with me, Cait."

Her heart gave a little leap. "Are you sure you aren't going to get sick of me? You have to work twelve to sixteen hours a day from now on."

He brought her hand to his lips, kissing it firmly. "I told you before, querida, I can't get enough of you. The crisis is past. I want—demand—the time to get to know you better. All I've got are bits and pieces and I'm not satisfied."

Her fears and uncertainty were dissolved by the vibrancy in his husky voice. She loved him, completely and unequivocally. Perhaps he felt something similar for her.

Chapter Eleven

SHORTLY AFTER RETURNING, Cait felt as if someone had given the site a new infusion of energy. She knew word traveled fast, and the men seemed to have a more positive attitude. She attributed it in part to the fact that supplies were being trucked in around the clock to make up for the lack created by Campos and Cirre.

Early Friday morning she found she had to fly into BA to give a deposition for a grand-jury indictment against Campos.

"Filipo," she called. Her secretary bobbed into the room expectantly.

"Try and get hold of Señor Tobbar. Señor Henning and I have to fly into BA this morning. Tell Señor Tobbar he's got the reins until I return. He can reach me at my apartment if he needs me for anything."

"Sí, Señora Monahan."

They had a long wait in BA before the hearing began. By three o'clock in the afternoon, it was clear they wouldn't be able to return to the site that night. Cait released the plane and pilot to fly some needed supplies back to Rio Colorado. Sensing her frustration, Louie gave her an understanding look as they sat together in the room, waiting to be called into the hearing. "Well, Rose, look at it this way. You can spend a weekend in BA and get some shopping done. I hear they have nice leather articles up on Calle Florida."

She gave a soft snort of disdain. "Just what I need, a pair of leather shoes or another leather purse."

"Do I detect some unhappiness, darlin'?"

Cait squirmed and recrossed her long, coltish legs. "No."

Louie grinned. "What you need is a good dose of Dominic."

Her eyes widened as she stared at him. "Dominic?"

"Is there an echo in here?"

She laughed. "I can't fool you, can I?"

"Nope. Never could. Mind you, though, not that you tried. He's a nice fellow, Rose. I'm glad to see you gettin' along with him."

"Yes," she answered hesitantly, feeling her pulse leap at the thought.

Her head was throbbing incessantly when the hearing was finally adjourned. It was five-thirty, and she wasn't even hungry, when Louie dropped her off at the apartment and he headed back to the Claridge House Hotel. She wandered dully through the empty rooms and absently ran a bath. Later, as she lay in the fragrant water, she became acutely aware of how lonely she had become since leaving the site. Was she missing Dominic's care and attention?

It had been a hectic week at the site, and she'd only had glimpses of him from time to time. Once at a midnight meeting with several other supervisors, she had caught his wistful look in her direction. Groaning, Cait wanted to forget it all, and after patting dry, she slipped into her black silk gown and crawled into bed. Swiftly the tiredness of the week, coupled with the grueling two-hour hearing, spiraled her into a deep sleep.

Her dreams were peaceful at first, but her heart began to pound strongly when she heard the gas platform creak and lurch beneath the impact of the load of steel I-beams as it slashed into the newly erected drilling tower. This time . . . this time Cait knew she would view the entire episode just as she had that morning off the coast of Indonesia. . . . There would be no retreat, no turning back.

Screams drifted from between the smashed girders. The platform shivered, and Cait was jerked backward by the platform boss as men rushed with pry-away bars, ropes and cables. She began to moan as she saw the bodies below it; so many lifeless puppets strewn like smashed straws in the wind. At first she couldn't make out which one was Dave. . . .

She became aware of the punctuating beat of the diesel engine, the powerful hum of the hoist cable as the boom swung back and forth to remove the debris to get to the last man . . . her husband. She was crying hysterically, hearing the beating sound becoming louder and louder, until finally it broke the spell of the nightmare . . . but only after she saw Dave being gently lifted from the twisted metal grave.

She moved restlessly, pulled awake by the continued beating sound. She moved off the bed, her eyes wide with the wildness of the nightmare still alive within her. It was the door . . . someone was knocking heavily at her apartment door. Her hair fell in disarray about her shoulders as she stumbled through the darkness and shakily opened it.

"Cait! My God, are you all right? . . ."

She felt Dominic's arms envelop her, and she collapsed against him, sobbing without restraint. He lifted her off her feet and carried her into the bedroom, holding her tightly against his body. Grimly he sat her down on the edge of the bed, soothingly reassuring her and stroking her hair in a gentle motion. He rocked her back and forth like a child, whispering small words of encouragement. "Sshhh, querida, it's all over . . . it's all right. You're safe . . . sshhh . . . I'm here. That's a good girl, try and take a deep breath . . . good . . ."

Cait clung to Dominic, her fingers digging into his chest as she tried to wrestle with the grief she had controlled for too long. His healing words only released that anguish and inner hurt, and she lay helpless against him, weeping until she had no more tears to cry. Her body shivered and shook, and she felt his arms tighten when she whimpered. Her eyes were wide and frightened as she continued to see her husband being brought to the main deck of the platform. Another cry broke from her, this one mirroring the utter helplessness and finality of the accident.

Dominic frowned, leaned over, watching her closely. His fingers brushed her temple and cheek in a protective gesture. "What do you see?" he demanded softly. "Tell me, querida."

"I—can't . . . oh, God . . . NO!" She buried her head, starting to sob all over again.

Firmly he pulled her hand away from her face and forced her to look up at him. "Cait, you've got to tell me what you see. You can't keep letting this night-mare hold you. Don't you understand? Talk about it, dammit!"

Her lips parted and trembled, and she stared past him at the darkened wall of the bedroom. Old fears raced through and left her speechless.

"Cait!" he breathed angrily. "I said tell me about it. Now!"

She swallowed convulsively, her body numb with shock. "I—see . . ."

"Describe it to me."

"They—oh, God, it's . . . Dave. Alive . . . he isn't alive." She choked and tried to stifle a moan.

"He's not alive?"

"No. Oh, how I wanted to see him alive . . ."

"Do you see him?"

She shuddered, her eyes bright with anguish. "What?"

Tears continued to trickle down her pale, drawn features as she stared unseeingly at the wall. "Half his face is torn away. He's dead!" she whispered, her voice flat.

"Oh, my God, Cait," he breathed, pulling her against him. "I'm so damn sorry."

She felt his hand massaging her neck, shoulders and back as she lay against him, concentrating on the steady, reassuring beat of his strong heart. Slowly her arms slid around his body, and she pressed her cheek against his chest in silent thanks. She clung wordlessly to him. She did not feel embarrassed at having shared the worst of the nightmare with him. He had under-stood. Her eyes darkened with confusion, and she cleared her throat. "Am I going crazy, Dominic?"

He pressed a kiss to her forehead. "No, querida. A nightmare is like a brief walk into reality during sleep. You couldn't accept something that horrible all at once."

"Every time I dreamed, I'd see more and more of the accident."

He sighed heavily and managed a small smile. "I wore my wounds on the outside, wreaking hell on other people. You"—he slid his fingers through her silken hair—"wore your wounds inside and tried to work them out through dreams."

"Will it ever end? What do I have to do to release it?"

He leaned over, a gentle smile on his mouth as he placed his finger beneath her chin and lifted her face to meet his amber gaze. "It ended tonight, querida. Never again will you have to relive it. Now it's part of the past, and it will stay there. The pain won't be so bad, either, and eventually you'll remember your husband without hurting. Only the good feelings and good memories will remain."

She managed to sit up, aware of his hand against her cheek. "How do you know all this?" she asked, her voice tremulous. She searched his eyes for the answer and saw only a tender flame within his lambent gaze.

"When Alicia divorced me, I thought it was the end of the world. It was a marriage arranged by my parents, and I was only nineteen, and so damn foolish." He shrugged. "I eventually fell in love with her so totally that when her infidelity was discovered, both families agreed that a divorce was the only solution."

"But you said you loved her. Couldn't you forgive her, Dominic?"

"I—yes, I would have . . . but she wanted to marry one of her lovers." He hesitated, the silence emphasizing his pain. "I couldn't keep her if she was unhappy."

Cait reached up, caressing his face. "It must have hurt terribly."

"No worse than watching Dave get killed, querida. Your pain came unexpectedly, and it's taken this long to work out the shock. Mine was a slow, painful death. I distrusted all women because of Alicia. I blamed all of them for what she had become." He leaned down, his mouth covering her lips in a tender, searching kiss.

Cait moaned, her arms instinctively slipping around his neck. She molded her body against him, feeling the hard strength of his muscles. She felt cleansed and whole, and a new flame stirred to life deep within her body, a shiver of passion ignited by the deepening exploratory kiss he was pressing upon her willing lips.

His strong fingers moved like liquid fire down her back, trapping her possessively against him. Slowly they parted, and Cait was aware of her heart clamoring against her breast like a caged bird straining for its freedom. She stared up at him in wonder, meeting his golden eyes. Her lips parted and she hesitantly reached out, her fingers brushing his generous mouth. He claimed her hand, squeezing it gently.

"I want to love you," he whispered huskily.

She closed her eyes, swaying against him in answer, a slender willow bending against a sturdy oak. Now Cait recognized the hungry light in his eyes. It was desire for her, and her alone. Somewhere in her spinning thoughts, she knew Dominic had waited until she had rid herself of the last vestiges of the past before bringing their physical bodies together in an act that could only mean a renewal of love. Something they both desperately recognized, wanted and were patient enough to wait and receive.

He gently laid her back on the bed, running his hand over her naked shoulder, down the side of her breast, to her flat stomach and the curve of her hip and long thigh. "God, you're beautiful," he breathed, leaning over, his mouth claiming her lips.

He tasted clean. Her tears were shared between them, tears spent in grief and claimed in love. Gladly she reached upward, pulling him down upon her yearning body. His fingers trailed down her back, making her shiver uncontrollably, moving now to cup her buttocks to pull her tightly to him. His stroking hand moved down her slender neck, pushing the strap of the negligee off her shoulder. Cait clung to his back in anticipation of his purposeful kisses, which began at the base of her throat.

Her skin grew hot and tight around each breast as his mouth sought out the valley between them. A small cry of pleasure broke from her as his lips nibbled insistently at the hardened peaks, and she moaned, arching her body demandingly against him, wanting...needing fulfillment more than she had ever thought possible.

She had never seen him naked, but now, in the weak moonlight that filtered through the window, she drew in a breath of utter delight. It seemed like agonizing hours before he had shed his clothes and returned to the bed, scooping her up in his arms and holding her tightly to him. Nuzzling him, Cait ran her fingers across the silken hair on his broad, well-muscled chest, down the steel length of his torso and lean waist. She felt him tense, a low groan coming from his throat, vibrating through her sensitive body. He could no longer remain quiescent, and Cait felt herself respond to the fiery heat she had kindled within him.

This time, as it was meant to be, Cait touched and stroked his body, as if it were a finely tuned instrument. But the fire flowing moltenly, achingly through her lower body had a life of its own, and she whimpered, begging him to complete the union, to make them one, as she had always desired.

"Yes," she whispered. "Oh, please, Dominic...yes..." His knee pressed between her straining thighs, parting them, his weight settling on top of her wet body.

"God," he whispered huskily, "so beautiful, so..."

She felt him hesitate, and she arched upward against him, a moan of momentary agony surfacing from her lips. His head rested against her neck and jaw, and she felt him leash his quivering body to protect her.

"Wait..." he whispered hoarsely.

"No...no!"

"God, I love you," he cried softly, and pulled her tightly against him as he slowly, deliciously urged her pulsating body into higher and higher circles of heady, mindless pleasure.

She felt him thrust inward savagely, demandingly, just as she had known he would. A rippling cry of satisfaction clawed up her throat as she felt the volcanic explosion racing up her spine like a jolting elec-

tric shock, numbing her conscious mind into a cloud
of exquisite joy. Tears trailed down her cheeks and
a tender smile touched her bruised, parted lips as she
felt Dominic tense. The growl of release from deep
within his throat made her flesh tingle.

Slowly, like the silence of dawn, Cait became
aware of familiar sounds around them. She rested her
fingers on the soft mat of black hair on his chest,
feeling the heavy thud of his heart against his ribs.
Smiling blissfully, she pressed her wet, tamed form
against him and felt his arms tighten into an embrace.
His rough, calloused hand moved down along her
arm, waist and hip in an unspoken gesture, and she
closed her eyes. Sleep claimed her, pulling her down
into a cottony world of cradled joy.

Sunlight stole softly into the bedroom, giving the
pale-lavender room a fragile radiance as light filtered
through the lace curtains, creating soft patterns on the
wall. Cait stirred, unconsciously pressing her length
against the man who still held her in his arms. Re-
calling the night before, she smiled, stretching like
a cat after a long, satisfying sleep. Dominic's arm
pulled her closer, and willingly she complied, content
to nestle her head beneath his chin. She moved her
fingers across his chest in a random careless gesture
and knew he had awakened. She closed her eyes as
he pressed his lips to her cheek.

Each touch communicated what words never could.
She had almost forgotten what it was like to run her
hand over a man's body and feel the muscles relax
or tense accordingly, and she gloried in that discovery.
More than anything else, she was ecstatic that Dom-

inic needed touching and holding just as much as she did. It pleased her, and she raised herself up on her elbow, her hair cascading across his chest as she gazed down into his amber eyes.

"You've given me life, do you realize that?" she whispered, meaning it in many ways.

She hoped he understood. Not only had he helped cleanse her old wounds, he had also showed her that she could respond as she had once before.

He reached up, capturing her chin and drawing her down until their lips met in a fragile kiss. Cait was hypnotized by the burning desire deep within his eyes as she drew only an inch away from his strong mouth. "It was a fair exchange, querida. You helped me discover a missing part to myself last night." He caressed her hair, allowing the silken tresses to slip through his fingers.

"What do you mean?"

"I never thought I could deeply love a woman again." He studied her intently, as if to memorize her face. "Do you have any idea how lovely you are? No, don't laugh, querida, I mean it. Dios, the first time I saw you, I thought I was going to lose myself in those sea-foam eyes of yours. It took everything I had, to keep from staring at you like a gawky young boy."

She smiled tenderly, tracing the outline of his mouth with her fingertip. "You scared the hell out of me the first time I saw you."

He laughed, the chuckle rumbling deep within his chest. "You hide your fears and wounds well, querida." He frowned. "Too well, in fact."

"Oh?"

"Yes. I know a side of you that is so damn sensitive and giving. That façade you throw up at work is a good one, but it can work against you, too. I worry about that."

Cait snuggled down into his arms, giving him a delicious hug of utter joy. "Well, if I roll over and play a woman, at the site, nothing will get done."

"One of these days, when the idea is accepted more, the women who follow you won't have to hide their womanhood, not ever." He kissed the crown of her head, giving her a quick squeeze.

"Listen, whatever was wrong with me is right now, believe me," she answered.

"Just what the doctor ordered?" he teased.

Cait shut her eyes momentarily. "God, that's the truth. I never realized how tense I was until—"

"Well," he murmured, pushing himself up and capturing her. "I'll just make sure you stay relaxed for the rest of this project."

She looked up at him, her eyes betraying the confusion she felt. "Dominic, where are we going?" she whispered.

He shrugged his broad shoulders and smiled indulgently, his hand trailing down her slender neck. "Keep your engineering rationale out of our relationship, mi leona."

She grimaced at his retort and tried to pull free. Within moments he had her gently pinned, and she was vividly aware of his barely restrained control. He leaned down, kissing her soundly.

"I don't know what you're talking about," she protested.

He grinned and nibbled at her earlobe. "Yes, you

do, querida. Engineers are raised on a pablum of logic, rationale and geometry. Just don't try and label what we have, what it is or where it's going, because you could destroy it with too much analysis." He trailed fiery kisses down her throat to her breasts. She arched instinctively. "Don't think, querida, just act and react," he growled huskily.

What little logical thinking she had done was explosively detonated in her dizzied, frenzied senses. Time became a throbbing whirlpool of lights, color and a rhythm of bodies matched in unison to each other. She had had no idea of how thirsty her body had become in those long months since her husband's death, and in glorious seconds of eternity, she became one with Dominic, a cry of pleasure bubbling from her throat. Afterward she lay against him, totally spent, and absolved of the past. Only the faint smile in his golden eyes mattered, and she returned that intimate smile, nuzzling her head against his neck and jaw.

Later, as the intensity of their shared passion ebbed like an outgoing tide, Cait noticed, for the first time, how high the sun had become.

"It's probably around ten," Dominic replied lazily.

"Sinful, isn't it?"

"Not in the least. Do you feel guilty?"

"No. I feel good."

"Are you hungry?"

"Not any more."

Dominic grinned. "I'm talking about food, querida."

"Oh. Well, yes, come to think of it, I'm starved."

"Me too. I have an idea."

"What?"

"Let's have breakfast at my ranch. It's only a thirty-minute flight from BA. What do you say?"

Cait frowned, and he tapped her on the nose. "Stop thinking about the damn site. It's fine."

She grinned, embarrassed. "Do you read minds too?"

"With special people, I do." He touched her mouth with his in a lingering kiss. "And you are very special, mi leona. Now, how about breakfast? I'll cook."

"You're on. I like scrambled eggs, in case you break the yolks."

He laughed fully, embracing her. "I haven't broken a yolk in two years."

Chapter Twelve

CAIT STARED DOWN at the two eggs in the frying pan. She muffled a giggle and stole a glance up at Dominic. "Well, one out of two isn't bad. I'll eat the scrambled one and you can have the good egg."

She leaned against him for a moment in laughter. "I really don't have a preference, master chef. I'll butter the toast."

"Mmm, good. Oh, bring the honey, it's in the refrigerator."

He put the plates down on a patio table beneath a silver-leafed eucalyptus tree. A high adobe brick wall surrounded the well-kept garden, and Cait inhaled the fragrant flowers.

"This is a lovely home, Dominic. Now I can see why you enjoy coming here."

He poured the coffee, and they sat down. "I'm here only three months out of the year at the most. The rest of the time I'm on projects."

Cait dug hungrily into the egg and took a bite of her toast. "It's so peaceful here. I love this garden."

"I knew you would. You have the earth in your soul, Cait Monahan."

"That and bulldozers." She laughed.

She felt more at peace than she had since Dave's death. Dominic made everything feel right. No matter where he was, she treasured being there with him.

The flight from BA had been spectacular, and she had gotten her first glimpse of the true pampas, or the Camp, as it was called. She had had no idea what the Camp would be like. The smell of freshly cut hay filled the air with a heady perfume, and Cait inhaled deeply as she leaned against the wrought-iron chair, holding her coffee cup close to her lips.

Dominic glanced over at her. "You like the smell too."

"Very much. It reminds me of my home in Colorado. Sort of makes me homesick."

"Home is where the heart is, querida."

She sipped the coffee, a glint in her emerald eyes. "Does being home make the philosopher in you come out?"

"Sometimes. Mostly it's the company I'm keeping. Do you always make a man want to confide in you?"

She colored slightly and set the cup down. "Dave and I always talked a lot about what we felt, saw or heard. Maybe that's it."

"It's a good habit to get into. I just wished that when I was younger, I had had the good sense to know that."

Cait toyed with the china cup. "I can't imagine any marriage surviving without a lot of honest communication."

He picked up her hand, giving it a light squeeze. "Well, let's talk. What do you want to do today? We don't have to be anywhere until late Sunday afternoon."

"I'd love to explore your ranch and see your famous gauchos, if that's possible."

He inclined his head. "All of that is possible, mi leona." They walked across the patio toward a side door that led into a maze of paddocks. Cait sized up the broodmares, with their young babies.

"They're thoroughbreds," Dominic explained. "Father imported most of the stock off Kentucky farms. When I married, he gave me most of the blood-stock, and I took over the breeding end of the operation."

"Did you enjoy it?"

He rested his darkly bronzed arms on the paddock. "I enjoyed the foaling. Watching those colts and fillies struggle to stand, minutes after they were born, has always fascinated me."

Cait laughed. "Dominic Tobbar, you are a big softy at heart. Why don't you let it show more?"

His eyes darkened, and he picked up her hand, continuing toward the barn. "Let's just say circumstances quenched some of my natural exuberance. But"—he looked down at her—"you seem to have a knack of bringing it out."

At the entrance Cait brightened. Horses neighed in greeting as they walked down the center aisle of the spotless rows of boxstalls. Dominic stopped at each one and introduced her to his charges. Finally, at the end, he slid open the door and lead a dainty bay mare out into the saddling area.

"This is Dirah. Do you recognize her breeding?"

Cait eyed the mare critically. She had a broad forehead, large, expressive black eyes and a dished face that sloped into a teacup muzzle. "Distinctly Arabian," she decided.

"Very good," he praised.

"Your favorite breed?"

Dominic lifted a blanket and saddle from the tack room and expertly saddled the mare. "Yes."

"Did your father approve?"

"No. But then, he never did approve of much of what I wanted. So what was the difference?" He bridled Dirah and put the reins in Cait's awaiting hand. "I wanted to breed Arabs with thoroughbreds to produce a better Camp horse, one with speed and endurance. The gauchos have always used those chunky little Spanish horses." He pulled a tall chestnut gelding from the next stall, and Cait could see the best traits of Arab breeding in the horse. Within minutes, Dominic had him saddled, and they led them out into the sunlight.

"Here, you'll need this," he said, handing her a hat that reminded her of the type horsemen in the bull arena wore. He gave her a dazzling smile. "Ready?"

Cait mounted in one smooth motion. The bay mare sidled in anticipation. "Ready," she answered.

The grass of the Camp lay in a carpet before them as they trotted away from the small ranch area. The movement of a good horse beneath her and the hot sun overhead made Cait doubly aware of her deep feeling for the natural world. Occasionally Dominic's leg brushed against her own, and she gloried in the slight touch. It seemed so natural, and the day seemed to belong only to them.

The knee-high grass gave way to shorter alfalfa and clover fields which had been recently cut. Long rectangular bales of hay lay in neat rows, reminding Cait of soldiers standing at rigid attention. Dominic halted, squinting toward the east.

"There, can you see it? That dust cloud?"

Cait pulled her mare to a stop and shaded her eyes. "Yes. What is it?"

"Let's head that way. That's where the gauchos are singling out the calves from their mothers."

They swung into a gallop, and the fields became a blur of green beneath the horses' pounding hoofs. Laughter sprang from Cait's throat as she moved in unison with each stride of the mare. Once she felt her horse tense, and spotted an armadillo dashing madly for the safety of his hole. Such holes could spell disaster for an animal, and she wisely followed Dominic, who seemed to know the safest route through the unfenced fields.

As they neared their destination, Dominic moved upwind from the clouds of dust created by the cows mooing plaintively for their recently removed calves. Holding pens made of maroon-colored fence posts kept the bawling babies away from the rest of the milling herds. Gauchos expertly swung their lassos to prevent single animals from breaking away from the main group.

They slowed to a stop, and Cait reached down to pat Dirah. Dominic swung his leg over the saddle and rested lazily atop the gelding. He waved to one gaucho and turned to Cait. "That's Giulio, the manager of this herd and majordomo over the rest of the gauchos. He's been with us since long before I was born."

Cait smiled, admiring the foreign flavor of the costume. She was used to cowboy hats, narrow-toed boots and long-sleeved shirts. Instead the gauchos wore a black beret tipped cockily to one side of their lean, spare features. The glint of metal drew her attention, and she asked, "What are they wearing around their waists?"

"Coins. It's a statement of a gaucho's total monetary worth. You can see it's a very wide belt, and most of them keep an assortment of items in it, including a *facón* or dagger. They use that to kill or skin an animal, to fight with or as a skewer over a fire to hold their meat. It's an all-purpose weapon."

"Is it true they are hot-tempered?"

Dominic shrugged. "Seventy years ago, they had a reputation for being fierce. Did you know they helped to build Argentina's independence? A long time ago, the word gaucho meant outcast or a lost animal. But ever since they rendered their services to General Martin de Guemes, they've been considered heroes. Without them, we'd have a monarchy. So the name became a compliment instead of an insult. These are men who live by a fairly simple code, mi leona. In the past they killed for honor or in the heat of passion—but never over money. Nowadays only the stories are passed on, and the men are a relatively tame lot."

"That's a shame."

Dominic grinned. "Do you think so? I don't think you'd like being married to one."

She returned the smile. "Why not?"

"For one, they used to live in mud-and-grass shacks. A bed was made up of animal skins, and a chair was constructed of a set of horse skulls or hip bones. Sometimes they'd find an ostrich egg or bring home *vizcachas* for a change of diet."

Cait wrinkled her nose. "What is a vizcacha?"

"A cross between a rat and rabbit, which grows to be about two feet long. It tastes pretty good, despite the ugliness of the thing." He laughed. "Back then, water was very scarce and the people never took baths. The women had to live in those huts, with little more than a shapeless gown to wear and no shoes."

"You're right, I'd never make a gaucho's woman."

"Watch that gaucho single out that calf," he said.

Cait straightened up in the saddle, watching the dust-caked horse and rider spurt out of the herd. The gaucho pulled the *boleadoras* from around his waist, swinging the two balls that were suspended from a long leather strap above his head. In an instant he had loosed the *bola*, and Cait watched in admiration as the calf went down, two of his legs wrapped expertly by the bola. "He's good," she admitted.

Dominic agreed. "On the plus side, a gaucho is probably one of the hardest-working professionals in Argentina. Gauchos are of Indian extraction, and no one can hunt, trap, trail and herd better than they can. I know that sounds chauvinistic, but that's their code."

Cait laughed. "You mean they wouldn't like me to go out there and rope one of those calves for them?"

"Not in the least. They think a woman's place is at home, raising the children."

She smiled, appreciating the timing of the gauchos' movements on their well-trained horses. Their baggy black trousers and rope-soled sandals looked strange, but Cait realized those wiry, high-cheeked men could probably outwork ranch hands from Colorado. "You seem to enjoy this sort of work."

Dominic lifted his leg over the gelding, and they

turned back the way they had come. "Yes, I do. Look, there's Giulio. He's been with us since before I was born, and he became a sort of foster father when I was very young. My real father had his business in BA, and I saw him only on weekends. I probably rode more with Giulio than I ever walked the first seven years of my life."

"When you talk about him, Dominic, I hear a special sound in your voice, almost as if you were back in that time."

He shrugged, reaching out to press a kiss to her hand. "Giulio made me see the difference between money and power, and what it was like to be my own person." He smiled, drinking in her attentive features. "And that's where the rub between my father and me began. I saw my mother alone five days of a week, sometimes more, because he was in the city. I saw Giulio ride back to his home every night, into the waiting arms of his wife and five children. At five years old I knew which lifestyle I wanted."

"Did you spend a lot of nights at Giulio's home?"

"Yes. Far too many, according to my father."

She returned his carefree smile and felt a surge of pride. "So when did the friction begin?" she asked.

"When it was time for me to go to a private school instead of the local school, where all my friends were. I should amend that. My father felt I shouldn't have friends among the poor, only among the rich and affluent." Dominic rubbed the back of his neck and gave her a rueful sidelong glance. "I found out very quickly that rich kids were shallow and manipulative, compared to the farm friends I grew up with."

Cait nodded and closed her eyes, languishing in the warming rays of the setting sun. Curtains of heat rose from the land like filmy drapes waving lazily in the breeze. Sharing the past with Dominic seemed natural, and Cait realized how much he had entrusted her with. It spoke of the seriousness of their relationship, and she felt a thrill of happiness. She watched him ride with an ease born of having done it all his life.

"I hear that nasty word again," she teased.

"Manipulate?"

"Yes. I thought you had grown to dislike the word, because of your marriage, but I can see now it happened much earlier."

He laughed. "And with that knowledge, you'd think I would have recognized those very traits in Alicia. But I didn't. I fell hopelessly in love with her. But I had no business getting married."

"You said it had been arranged?"

"Yes. It was the *only* thing I let my father ever talk me into, and what a disaster it turned out to be. After the divorce he grudgingly acknowledged I was the best one to run my life. I know he feels responsible and guilty for shoving the marriage on me."

Cait noticed a slight tremor in his voice when he said "Alicia." A tiny alarm went off in her head, and she frowned. "For all the problems she seems to have caused, you sound as if you still love her." It was posed as a statement, but Cait felt the question in her own unsure voice.

She looked intently at Dominic and found herself melting each time she took in his strong face and golden eyes, each time she felt the strength of his hard, muscular body against her own. She sighed, her heart thudding.

"I hated her for a long time, Cait. And until very

recently it seemed I was still attracted to that kind of woman. That's why I had a hell of a time with you. None of the women I knew, would ever dream of laughing freely or crying openly. When I made love to them, it was like making love to a carefully timed machine that was rigged to make the proper response or the proper rejoinder at the proper time." He studied her. "Now do you understand why I blundered in so brazenly with you at the beginning? You were so damn lovely, and I couldn't believe my eyes. All I knew was that I wanted you. All my usual lines back-fired with you." They laughed.

"I was absolutely mortified at your insolence! I thought this couldn't be happening—not on my job!"

"You changed me, though, querida."

Cait leaned across the saddle, her lips touching his strong, sun-warmed mouth. "No more than you gave me life, darling . . ." she whispered tremulously.

"I have a surprise for you," he said. "Let's stop and give the horses a well-earned rest. It's time for a siesta, and all gauchos halt their work and make maté now."

Cait dismounted, loosened the hat she wore and placed it on the saddle horn. There were no trees in sight for as far as she could see, only the gently waving grass. Dominic hobbled both horses, cleared a spot in the ground, dug a small hole, and placed some bits of dried grass beneath a few lumps of charcoal. Cait sat cross-legged upwind from the small fire.

"You didn't tell me you were a boy scout," she teased.

Dominic brought the saddlebags over and laid them by Cait. "I'm not. I used matches, not a flint. Here, this is for you." He handed her an oblong gourd that had been hollowed out. It was delicately surrounded by filigreed silver at the base and sported an elegant handle. "No one," he instructed seriously, "should ever drink yerba maté without a gourd and *bombilla*, or straw. It is the custom of Argentina to provide guests with just such equipment, but nowadays, except when it is a very special person, maté is served in a china cup, with a saucer."

Cait marveled at the beauty of the gourd, which fit comfortably between her hands. "It's lovely, Dominic. But what do I do with it?"

He poured water from the canteen into a well-used, blackened teakettle that he placed above the fire on a hook suspended from an iron stake in the ground. He sat back on his heels, satisfaction lining his face. "It's about time you got steeped in the customs of Argentina, mi leona. Very few foreigners experience this custom. Here, crumble this small handful of maté into the bottom of your gourd."

Cait cautiously sniffed the dark-green leaves and did as she was instructed. "I feel like I'm going through an initiation ceremony." She laughed.

"In a sense, you are. A very pleasant one, however. Here, the water's beginning to boil. Set the gourd down and watch what happens . . ."

The water hit the bottom of the gourd, and a frothy green foam erupted and spewed over the sides. Cait wrinkled her nose. "Is it safe to drink?"

He poured his own, returning the kettle to the hook and adding more water. "I know it doesn't look very appetizing. Just add a teaspoon of sugar to it."

Cait stirred the maté, watching the foam slowly subside. She copied Dominic as he put his bombilla into the tea, and took her first tentative sip. Surprised, she declared, "It's not so bad."

"Good. Now come here and sit by me. I have a fable to tell you."

She slid into his awaiting embrace, amazed at how well their bodies always seemed to fit together. The sun was dipping closer to the horizon, and the bright whiteness of the day was dissolving into faint rose.

"Do you know what you did by drinking the maté?" he murmured.

"No," she replied huskily, her pulse leaping crazily at the base of her neck.

"Whether you know it or not, querida, you are now part of Argentina's soul. There is an old Indian legend involving Caa Iari, who is the spirit of all *yerbales,* or yerba maté trees and groves. Many hundreds of years ago, an old couple had a very, very beautiful daughter, and the love they held for her made them flee to the safety of the forest to protect her from marauding tribes. Unknown to them, a god disguised as a foot-weary traveler asked the old man and woman for food and housing for the night. Naturally they complied, and when the god discovered their undivided loyalty to the girl, he made the daughter immortal. Her spirit now resides in all maté groves, which she guards dutifully. When people drink yerba maté, she erases the hunger or pain they feel, and enables them to face all adversaries and dangers with courage. All who drink will come back to her land without fail." He leaned down, kissing Cait's cheek tenderly. "So you see, you are now my prisoner. I've tricked you into staying in Argentina."

Cait smiled and sipped more of the fragrant tea. "At least for the duration of the project, huh?"

Dominic laughed, his arm tightening around her. "Longer than that if the maté legend is true, querida."

Her pulse quickened. She was too content to explore the hidden meaning of his whispered words. The silence lengthened between them, and she finished the last of her yerba maté, setting the gourd down before them. Dominic massaged her shoulders, and she leaned back in response.

"You're just like a cat," he growled, "arching against my touch. Tell me, are you getting hungry?"

"Very much." She grinned, turning to meet his open gaze. "I like scrambled eggs."

Dominic managed a sour smile, getting to his feet and then lifting her from her sitting position. She settled against his fragrant male body, content to stare pensively into his golden eyes. "I had something more than eggs in mind. Like I said, it's time you were properly introduced to Argentina. Tonight I'm going to make *empanadas*. You can help if you want."

She grinned. "I wouldn't miss this for the world."

They rode back toward the fiery crimson-and-saffron-colored sunset, meeting several dusty gauchos on tired horses at the juncture of the hay fields and the long-stemmed pampas grass. By the time they reached the stable, Cait was starving. After unsaddling their mounts and rubbing them down, they locked arms and walked to the coolness of the small house.

After a quick hot shower, Cait joined Dominic in the kitchen. Her dark hair fell loosely about her shoulders, and he leaned down, kissing her mouth with delicious slowness. She broke away, laughing. "I thought you were hungry!"

He grinned, releasing her and putting two onions

in her hands. "I am. Come on, you chop the onions and I'll throw the rest of this together. How are you at rolling out pastry dough?"

Over two hours later Cait lay with Dominic in front of the fireplace, on a rug of spotted llamas' wool. The warmth of the flames lulled her into a blissful doze, and she leaned back into his cradling arms, thoroughly content. Darkness had followed quickly on the heels of the glorious sunset, and now, in the late fall, approaching winter was sweeping down off the mighty Andes, rapidly cooling the flat pampas.

Dominic leaned forward, his mouth brushing her robed shoulder. "Happy?" he murmured.

"Mmm, very," she answered drowsily. She closed her eyes, nestling against his broad shoulder. "If anyone had told me happiness like this was possible I would have said that was crazy."

"Me too."

Cait smiled; Whatever it was—and she knew it was love—was working the same spell upon Dominic. "What had you imagined as a future yourself?" she asked softly.

"Loneliness interspersed with work."

"Me too."

It was his turn to chuckle. "Are we opposite bookends?"

"No, we're just pessimistic about—" She was suddenly afraid to say it...to say that one four-letter word that had made her world change from shades of gray to brilliant rainbow hues.

"Cat got your tongue?" he teased, nibbling playfully on her earlobe. "I never thought that would happen."

Cait grinned, pulling away. "Then you say it," she challenged.

Dominic captured her hand and pulled her toward him. "Say what?" he returned huskily. "That you make my day seem lighter and my night a fantastic dream?" He kissed her palm, looking up into her emerald eyes.

Her heart thudded strongly.

"I don't feel like a prisoner any more," she whispered, leaning down and finding his waiting arms.

"Never again," he promised, covering her lips with a gentle exploratory kiss.

His moist breath fanned across her face, and she touched his mouth tenderly, tasting the bitter sweetness of the wine on his lips. In an almost lazy gesture, he nibbled her ear, placing small nips down the slender expanse of her neck to her throat. As he pulled the robe away with maddening slowness, she knew without a doubt she had never experienced such urgency as he was provoking within her now.

His entire body tensed and quivered as she rolled back, fitting herself against his frame, thrusting her hips forward to meet him. Dominic growled, his eyes narrowing, his breath harsh as he pinned her beneath him. "I want you," he said thickly, his mouth claiming her parted lips in a bruising, plundering kiss.

Cait felt the last vestiges of the silken robe being jerked impatiently from her arms, and she made a small mewing sound of contentment as she reached up, pulling him against her. His hands caressed her taut, expectant breasts, and he leaned over, tasting the salty velvetness of her heated skin.

Cait moaned, arching upward, her fingers digging into his steel-like shoulders, her body trembling with anticipation...with longing so intense that a slow ache began throbbing throughout her. His mouth sought her own, his tongue exploring the depths of her and tangling victoriously with her own. His other hand glided tantalizing down her form, across her hip bone, sliding between her waiting thighs.

This time she didn't want him to be gentle or hesitant, as he had been before. This time she wanted to experience the uncontrolled power of Dominic. "Take me..." she whispered huskily, gripping his powerful shoulders. "Now...please, don't wait..."

Her skin was wet with expectancy, her body strained against the tempo of his own. His entire being claimed her triumphantly. Her lashes fluttered against her cheekbones as he thrust deeply into her. A cry of pleasure broke from her lips, and she gloried in the brutal strength that indelibly stamped them both in that frenzied moment. Lightheaded pleasure drove her into higher and higher circles of ecstasy. Moments melted together and fused in a long, shuddering climax.

Cait quivered, held tightly within Dominic's embrace for long moments afterward. Damp hair lay against her rosy, flushed cheek, and he gently pushed it away, tucking it behind her ear. "I never thought," he whispered hoarsely, "it could ever be like this...not in a million years..."

She nodded mutely against the curve of his neck. Her fingers trailed down the bulging muscles of his upper arm to his hand, which rested heavily against her thigh. She could feel the blood coursing strongly through each vein, hear the heavy thud of his heart within his massive chest. "I love you," she murmured softly. She felt him shift, carefully depositing her on her back against the llama skins, an inquiring light in his turbulent gaze.

"I wasn't hearing wrong?" he asked, cupping her face in the palm of his large hand.

Cait barely shook her head, staring lovingly up into his boyish, relaxed features. "No . . . you heard right. I—I knew it a long time ago," she admitted, her voice barely above a whisper. "The past, darling . . . I had to work through the past first. You helped me let it go, and now I'm free . . . free to feel and love again. And I love you so much that my heart aches."

Dominic's features clouded with tenderness, and he groaned, crushing her in a smothering embrace. "Querida, you *are* my life . . ." he rasped thickly. "From the moment I saw you in the airport, I knew."

Sometime later, in her drowsy half-awake state, she felt Dominic lift her from the rug and carry her into the bedroom. To feel his strong, possessive arms pull her against him, to sleep beneath the goose-down quilt, stirred up something she had missed acutely— sleeping with a man she loved.

Chapter Thirteen

THEY RELUCTANTLY FLEW back to the work site, early Sunday evening. Cait watched the sun disappear beneath rapidly building clouds.

"Looks like a pretty well-developed cold front," Dominic said, as if reading her thoughts.

She nodded. "I hope it comes and goes in a day's time so it doesn't drop very much rain at the site."

He trimmed the tab on the plane. "I saw it barely on the horizon Friday night when I flew to BA to find you. A slow front means more rain than either one of us wants to think about."

"Those cofferdams . . ." she began, and then didn't finish the thought aloud.

"There's a lot of green concrete in the base slab pier," he said, "but it should stand the stress of a twelve-inch rise on the Rio Colorado." He reached out, brushing her cheek gently. "Stop worrying, querida."

Cait caught his hand and kissed it. "Now will you tell me what 'querida' means?"

"That's 'darling' in Spanish. Do you like it?"

Her green eyes darkened, and she murmured softly, "I love it, Dominic. Never stop calling me that."

He grinned, squeezing her shoulder. "I'm going to start calling you 'worry-wart' if you don't stop looking at that approaching front as if it were some kind of monster coming to devour our site."

All too soon they had landed. Pedro met them at the airstrip. Cait sat in the pickup between the two men and felt the torn edges of a strange new fear eating away at her. Dominic walked her slowly to the door of her quarters. He made no move to touch her or to kiss her; they had already agreed that at the site, no one was to suspect their relationship. It would not be good for morale.

"Getting up early tomorrow?" he asked, his voice a purr that sent shivers up her spine.

"Yes."

He smiled lazily, drinking in her features. "You're beautiful in the last rays of dusk, mi leona. Too bad Pedro is thirty feet away and watching us, or I'd steal one last kiss. I'll pick you up at five, and we'll grab an early breakfast over at the cook's trailer."

She allowed the warmth of his voice to cloak her. "Sounds fine. Good night..."

"I'll miss you in bed tonight, querida. Good night..."

She tossed and turned and slept poorly. The dreams that had once haunted her never came. Instead a nagging fear kept her awake most of the night. At five o'clock, it began to rain.

The honk of the horn outside her quarters made her heart pound faster. Just the thought of being near Dominic made her hurry to pick up a roll of blueprints and her briefcase. The headlights stabbed into the blackness of the morning as she dashed for the vehicle. Dominic threw open the door and she climbed in, shaking off the water from her rain slicker. Before she could push away a wet strand of hair, she found herself pulled into his arms, his mouth, warm and strong, sliding across her parting lips in a tender, passionate kiss.

"There," he growled, setting her on the seat beside him. "That's how much I missed you."

Wordlessly Cait touched her lips, staring at him.

He grinned and put the truck in gear. "Ready for a hard day's work?"

She returned the grin. "With that kind of start, of course I am."

Louie arrived at eight, and Cait called a meeting of all supervisors for an update on the project. Slowly she swung into a routine that gave her confidence. By late afternoon, reports were coming in of flooding in the low-lying areas where more and more portable pumps were being used so that work could continue. Toward nightfall, Cait grew worried as reports from upriver became more and more ominous—the water level was rising at an unprecedented rate. It meant that the newly constructed cofferdams would be subject to extreme pressure. By ten o'clock that night, Cait, swathed in a hard hat, rain gear and knee-high rubber boots, was down at the bridge-building area to personally check out the situation.

As she slogged awkwardly through ankle-deep muck, a small alarm went off in her head—Louie and Dominic had mentioned that a subcontractor had been suspected of cheating on the specs. Frowning and pushing the water away from her glistening face, Cait moved carefully to the lip of the bridge pier cofferdam. Several men with flashlights and portable lamps were down within the bridge pier form, checking the newly placed concrete.

A rise of bile in her throat made her mouth taste bitter and metallic. Her heart began pounding in her breast, and she clutched at her raincoat in reaction, panic driving a stake into her heart. Dominic! Her mind wheeled and screamed. Her eyes widened in horror as she recognized him down among the freshly placed formwork. She stifled a scream and began to back away from the cofferdam, her senses sheared by a growing monster of fear.

"Señora?" a worker queried, watching her strangely.

She had to contain the fear! Cait forced herself to halt. She was gasping like a fish pulled out of water. Leaning down, she forced the blood to rush back to her head and then unsteadily straightened up. "Get—" The acid bile stung her mouth, and she gagged, turning away. No! She couldn't vomit! What was wrong with her?...Oh, God, something was terribly wrong. She slid, nearly falling down the muddy enbankment. The worker's hand steadied her elbow.

"Cait!" Dominic's voice broke through the roar of the fear and the scalding pound of rain. She whirled, precariously off balance as she saw him jogging steadily toward her. The worker gave a quick nod and released her to Dominic's charge.

"My God, what's the matter? I saw you up at the top and you looked like you were going to faint! Cait?" He handed the heavy flashlight to his gang boss and grabbed her by the arms, forcing her to face him. "What's wrong?" he asked urgently.

She stared wordlessly up at him, her lips parted, trembling. She was shaking uncontrollably. If it weren't for his strength, her knees would have buckled uselessly beneath her. "I—don't—"

Dominic jerked his head to the left. "Dolph, get a truck up here—now!"

She uttered a moan, her body crumpling against him. The fear had taken control, and she felt helpless in its grip. Vaguely she felt herself being lifted into the truck, lying heavily against Dominic's hard, protective body.

Later, at the base camp, he walked her into her quarters and stripped off her rain gear, forcing her to lie down on the cot while he arranged blankets around her. The nakedness of the single lightbulb made the scene surrealistic as the drumming staccato of rain pierced her struggling consciousness. She felt panic returning when he left her side for a moment.

"Here," he ordered, lifting her head and cradling her against his shoulder, "drink this." He placed a tin cup to her lips, and she drank the liquid obediently.

Cait gasped, struggling to sit up as the rank whiskey plunged down her throat into her knotted stomach. He touched her hair wordlessly, his eyes worried.

"Better, querida?" he asked softly.

She managed a mechanical nod, drawing her knees up to her chin, closing her eyes. "Oh, God—Dominic, I don't know what happened..." Her voice cracked and she sobbed, burying her head against her knees. He raised himself onto the small bed and took her in his arms, whispering soothing, healing words. His warm breath fanned across her cheek and neck, and Cait wrapped her arms around his middle, crying softly.

Finally she was able to halt the tears and talk coherently. She lay in his arms, shaking her head in confusion. Dominic leaned over, kissing her cheek tenderly.

"Was it physical?" he questioned. "Are you running a temperature? When was the last time you had a malaria shot?"

"No...it's not physical." She cleared her aching throat, sitting up. He handed her the tin cup.

"Take another swallow," he urged.

She wrinkled her nose but managed another small gulp, shivering from the effects of it.

"You said it was fear?"

"Yes..." She looked up at him miserably. "I—I feel so stupid and helpless. I don't know what caused it. I didn't even feel it coming on. I had just climbed up to the cofferdam and was looking at the sheet piling...I saw the men..." Her eyes narrowed. "Wait...it happened when I saw you! The cofferdam looked like a coffin!"

He grinned, caressing her arm. "Isn't that going a bit far?" he teased.

She managed a small laugh that she did not feel. "Why would I have that sort of reaction?" she asked.

He embraced her tightly. "Maybe it's premarriage jitters."

Cait twisted free, her lips parted in disbelief. "Marriage?" she whispered.

"I don't like the idea of sleeping alone," he said,

smiling. "One night without you is one too many. Will you?"

She simply stared up into his golden eyes, wrapped in the secure warmth of his love. He kissed her full on the lips. "Well," he prodded, pulling only an inch away. "Will you marry me, Cait Monahan?"

"Yes, oh, yes!" She threw her arms around him, hugging him joyfully.

He laughed and patted her gently. "Good. Two weeks from now. After this damn rain stops. How about it?"

"But...your father...relatives..." she sputtered.

"It will be a small wedding, consisting of close family and friends," he stressed soberly. "People who like and love us for us, not for what they think we should have been, querida."

"I know my mom and dad will fly down. Oh, they'll be so happy for us, Dominic."

Already she felt much better, and insisted on going back to the office to work. They drove down to a warehouse near the bridge-building site and set up an emergency office there. Dominic checked the bridge area while Cait handled calls and gave directions to the workers. A few hours later, he returned, taking off his hard hat and shaking the excess water off his raincoat.

"What's it look like down there?" she wanted to know.

"Holding. But I just talked to Alverez, who is fifty miles upriver, and he says another two inches is on its way."

"What about those tie-backs?"

"They look okay at this point. Louie told you about the specs not meeting criteria?"

"Yes." She took off her hard hat, placing it on the plyboard table and then crossing her arms, thinking about the multiple problems that could occur. She met his golden eyes as they stared at each other across the room. The rain hitting the tin roof made an unrelenting din, and Cait could smell the brackish water from the river on him and his muddy boots.

"We could flood the cofferdam, but that would set us back weeks," she offered.

"I think we'd better put a twenty-four-hour watch on the cofferdams and bridge work and keep tabs on those tie-backs on an hourly basis."

She agreed. "Still, if something lets go, with this torrential rain, we won't be able to maneuver equipment or trucks to make a recovery. Look at this latest weather report—the front is now stationary and won't start moving off the area for at least another thirty-six hours."

Dominic swore, and ran his fingers through his dark wet hair. "Great. Any other good news?"

"No. Look, you organize the watch and I'll get the cook to provide food for the crews."

"Okay. How about taking a break and having a cup of coffee with me after that?"

She warmed at the suggestion. Just being near him was enough to make her feel vibrantly alive. "Yes . . . I'd like that."

He was just about to lean over and kiss her when Dolph opened the makeshift office door and poked his meaty face inside. "Herr Tobbar, the crew is ready. You want to instruct them?"

Dominic gave her an intense, silent look and then turned away. "Yeah. Let's get down there. Cait, I'll see you in about forty minutes."

The next day dragged slowly by, the gray landscape turning into a yellowish mire of mud. Hourly reports called in from upriver kept Cait abreast of the situation. Crews worked in twelve-hour shifts, sandbagging the banks of the swollen Rio Colorado as its crimson water overflowed the banks into areas where work had to be halted.

It was a necessary part of Cait's job to inspect problems that were now occurring all over the site. Dominic never left her side, sometimes glancing worriedly in her direction as she moved slowly through three inches of mud.

She could not logically pinpoint the fear she had felt the night before. Even without sleep, she felt good now. She moved around the base camp, sending words of encouragement to the weary workers.

They rested momentarily in the truck, silently watching the rain. The radio crackled to life, and Dominic answered the call.

"It's Dolph. He's getting worried about those tie-backs. Let's go down and investigate."

Sighing, she agreed, put the truck in gear and crept along the now washed-out road toward the distant river.

"Is this rain ever going to end?" she muttered.

He reached over, touching her shoulder. "I'm wondering too. Listen, you've got to get some sleep, querida. I'll play watchdog after we check out the tiebacks, and you get back to your quarters and grab six hours. When you wake up, I'll hit the sack for another six. This rain is going to hang around at least another day and a half."

Cait groaned. "Sleep, I could use. Okay, sounds fine. God, I hope those tie-backs hold. If they don't... Do you realize the entire side of that hill will slide down into that one cofferdam, smashing the sheeting, and then the river will crash into it and finish off the job?"

His lips hardened. "Only too well. Dolph knows what he's doing. He can spot a stress crack at a hundred yards, and right now he's babysitting up there on that hill. He'll let us know."

Trudging up the hill, sliding and falling several times, they finally stood at the long rectangular tieback section that stood fifty yards above the river. The cables were anchored tautly back into the earth at one end. The other anchor held the concrete retaining walls. Dolph broke into gutteral German that only Dominic understood. Cait stood by, waiting for him to interpret.

"Dolph says the earth is almost soaked to its saturation point. That means the ends of those tie-backs may be weakening from the increased force." He ran his fingers across the smooth gray surface.

Cait moved to the next tie-back, running her fingers over the area. She looked at Dominic. "Let's get a portable stress unit up here and measure each one. I don't like this."

He blew out a long breath, his hand resting tensely

on his hip. Cait followed his worried gaze down to
the cofferdam directly below them. "Yeah, let's do
that. You call it in. I'm going down there to check
out that sheeting one more time..."

She was about to agree when a spasm of fear trembled within her. She watched him slip and slide back
down the hill. A clawing sensation seared her throat,
and she lurched forward, her face whitening with
shock.

"No!" she screamed, reaching out in Dominic's
direction.

He had not heard her strangled cry. She watched
in horrified fascination as he lumbered down to the
cofferdam, entering it on the land side.

Her breath came in sharp, unrelenting sobs. She
heard Dolph's booming voice over the staccato of
rain. She dropped to her knees, a cry lodged in her
throat, just as Dominic turned and looked back up the
hill. His features tensed and he spun around, climbing
back to where she had fallen.

She was breathing in halting gasps as he reached
her side. His pale face tightened as he lifted her to
her feet. "Cait? What's wrong? What *is* it?"

Her fingers clawed convulsively at his yellow
slicker, her eyes wide and frightened. "Don't go—
no—" she cried hysterically. "You'll be killed...you
can't go down there...no..."

Miserably Cait stole a look at Dominic, who sat
on the stool, his elbow resting on the blueprint table.
She clasped her hands together in her lap, feeling
sapped and guilty.

"I'm sorry," she whispered painfully.

"Don't be . . ." He roused himself, coming over and kneeling in front of her, taking her muddied hands within his. "Cait, querida, that fear is from the past. That cofferdam resembles a gas platform in some ways, or at least the cavern that they pulled Dave out of. Your mind sees that and you lose control . . . you're going back to the time he was killed . . . re-experiencing the horror, the terribleness of his death. You see that now, don't you?" The urgency in his voice brought scalding tears to her eyes, and she sniffed, wiping them awkwardly away with the back of her hand.

"Y—yes, I do now. Oh, God, Dominic, every time I see you going into that—that—coffin I—I lose control of myself." Her voice became strained, haunted. "I love you too much to lose you—do you see that?"

"No—no, Cait. You aren't going to lose me, for God's sake. That sheeting isn't going to break. I'm as safe there as on land. You know that, dammit. You're an engineer. You understand the built-in stress factors as much as I do." He grabbed her by the arms, shaking her gently. "The logical part of your mind knows that."

"Yes!" she cried, breaking his hold and standing up. "Of course I know that! But I don't know it here!" She pointed to her heart, her eyes large with fear. "I don't want to lose you, Dominic!"

He rose slowly, watching her grimly. "Look, it's been almost thirty hours since you slept. I'm taking you back to the camp and you're going to sleep."

Chapter Fourteen

WHEN CAIT AWOKE seven hours later, Pedro drove her back to the office. Louie roused himself as she entered.

"Go back to sleep, Louie. I'll work in the other office."

He smiled grimly, yawning. "No way, darlin'. Besides, I got a five-minute cat nap just now, and feel better than ever."

Cait managed a small smile, riffling through the messages and reports from all parts of the drowning site. Louie looked at her closely. "For someone who's supposed to be in love, you ain't lookin' too good, Rose. What's wrong?"

Cait jerked her head up and stared at him. "Who told you?" Her voice was brittle, almost accusing.

"Dom told me," he said quietly. "Rose, darlin' . . . relax, will you?"

"I suppose he told you about my—my fear?" she snapped.

"No—no, he didn't. He just said you were edgy and needed some sleep. Hey," he remonstrated gently, rubbing her shoulder, "this is Louie, your friend, re-member? Rose, what's eatin' at you? Come on, darlin', let it out..."

"If I *really* loved him, Louie, I would take his word that he'd be safe down there in the cofferdam. But I can't! God, I just can't, and it's not that I don't love him enough!" Her voice was filled with anguish. "I love him so much it hurts! I—I've *never* loved anyone so hard in my life—not even Dave. With Dave it was like living with a quiet, peaceful pool. Dominic is like an ever-changing ocean...he's so wonderful. Oh, Louie, what am I going to do? How am I going to control this fear and at the same time convince him I really do love him enough to overcome it?"

"Just by the fact that you recognize the problem and *want* to cope with the situation. Neither of you knew it was going to happen like this, darlin'." He shook her gently, a smile edging the corners of his thin mouth. "And don't you dare think that he's going to stop loving you just because of this silly quirk."

She got up slowly, wrapping her arms around her-self. A terrific gust of wind hit the side of the office trailer, making it shudder like a wounded beast. "Louie, I'd better get back on the job...assess the damage. Do you know where Dominic is?"

"Last I heard, he was at the warehouse, darlin'. Get yourself down there. You'll be a sight for sore eyes to him, I know."

By the time she staggered into the makeshift office, Cait was soaked to the skin. Dominic was on the field phone when she entered the small room filled with men huddled around the potbellied stove.

A small path was made for her, and she forced a

smile for the men's benefit. Dominic's head lifted, his gaze meeting hers. He wearily replaced the receiver. Pushing wet strands of black hair off his forehead, he muttered, "Those damn tie-backs are weakening..."

Cait's face tightened and paled. "And the hill? What's the consistency of the earth?"

Dom looked up, his eyes hungrily taking in her entire body. "Completely saturated."

"Damn," she swore softly, clenching her fist. "What's the last weather report?"

"Rain will end in another six hours. You can feel the temperature dropping, so the front's gone by, thank God."

"River level?"

He managed a sour smile, turning around on the stool and resting both arms on his thighs. "It really doesn't matter any more. We're at twenty inches, and expecting three more before it's all over."

"And the cofferdams?" She could barely get the words out.

"The PZ-38's are standing up to it. I have a crew going down every thirty minutes to monitor the condition of the green concrete and shoring."

Her heart was thudding dully in her breast. "All right"—her voice quavered audibly—"let's go up there. I want to see it for myself."

Dominic looked at her strangely, opened his mouth to say something and then shut it. He shrugged into his rain slicker and threw on his hard hat. Turning to Dolph he said, "You and the boys stay here and warm up. Send men down two at a time when your break is over."

"Ja," Dolph agreed.

Cait said nothing as she got in on the passenger side of the truck, letting Dominic drive. It was cold.

"You all right, Cait?"

She jumped and turned, staring at him. "Y—yes . . . the temperature."

He put the truck in gear and they crawled through the shrouded morning light toward the river. "Did you get some sleep?" he asked.

"Yes. Did you?"

"No. Things fell apart right after you left." He managed a grin. "Nothing goes right without you around, *querida*. Not a damn thing." He reached over, clasping her hand and giving it a hard squeeze. "You know I'm going to have to go down in that cofferdam."

It was a statement, not a question. "Yes," she answered rawly, "I know."

Her eyes sought out the reddish hill above the cofferdam, trying to estimate the ability of the tie-backs to hold the thousands of tons of wet earth in place.

"Why can't you send your workmen down there to check for you?" she squeaked.

"Would you?" he returned gently.

Cait hung her head, tears scalding her eyes. "No—you're not a very good leader if you can't do it yourself. . . ."

He braked the truck and turned off the engine. Reaching out, he drew Cait to him, his strong mouth seeking the softness of her lips. A small cry echoed in her throat as he kissed her longingly. It was a tender, eternal kiss that left her breathless. He studied her face as if to impress it in his memory one last time. . . .

"We'll do it together," he whispered huskily. "Come on..."

He kept a firm grip on her elbow as they climbed the gooey hill of earth, both panting as they reached the crest. The tie-backs stared mutely back at them, and Dominic raised his chin, his eyes narrowed, gauging the potential of the soil to push the concrete slabs over on them. Rain slashed cruelly at their faces, and Cait ducked her head, shielding her eyes from it with her other arm. Her heart pounded unrelieved in her chest, and her throat ached with unshed tears, as they cautiously made their way along the temporary scaffolding to inspect the tie-back anchors.

"Here..." Dominic rasped, and pulled out a small flashlight to look for obvious stress cracks in the cable buttons.

Cait held her breath as he carefully checked each of them. "Well?"

"No change."

She drew in a deep breath. "Good."

"Move on down. The second one is two ties over," he ordered. Her foot suddenly slipped, and a small cry was torn from her throat. She felt Dominic's vise-like grip on her shoulder as he hauled her back from the edge. Trembling, she gulped in air.

"All right?" he breathed, holding her tightly.

Her voice was unsteady. "Y—yes. Hurry. Let's get this over with...."

"Damn," he growled, inspecting the second anchor point. "It contains ten button failures and twelve obviously overstressed points."

He hurried her along the small scaffolding, inspecting each of the remaining anchors, until they were safely away from the potential landslide area.

Planting his fists on his hips, he studied the situation, glancing first at the hill and then at the cofferdam. He looked at his watch and then over at Cait.

"I have a plan. If this baby does decide to go, we might, just might have a chance of saving that cofferdam."

"But how?"

"I should have thought of this earlier! Come on. Let's hurry. I need to get to a radio."

She sat in the cab, shivering, her arms wrapped around her as she listened to the excitement in Dominic's voice. He was calling up four D-9 Cats to begin shoving tons of earth away from the top of the crest tie-backs, thereby alleviating some of the downward gravity-pressure of the soaked soil. It might then relieve the tie-backs and, if they were lucky, everything would remain intact. . . .

He hung up, grinning broadly, and gave her a sound kiss. "See what happens when you're around? I get the most inventive ideas."

She managed a small smile. Some of her fear was beginning to abate. His lowered voice broke into her careening thoughts. "Are you ready, Cait?"

Her heart plunged into the pit of her stomach, and her mouth went suddenly dry. He was going down there . . . down from where he might never return. She turned, her eyes filled with agony as she looked across the distance. Her heart thundered "no!" but her mind said, "Go with him. . . . Prove your love and trust in him. . . . He wouldn't go down there if it weren't reasonably safe."

"We can do it," he coaxed softly. "Together, Cait. Now . . ."

She could barely hear the rain for the roaring of blood through her skull as they carefully made their way down the steep embankment. Her knuckles whitened as she gripped his forearm to stop from slipping. God, she *had* to trust his decision...had to go on...go down there. He wasn't going to be killed by the landslide. No. Cait's darkened gaze swung skyward to the heavily laden clouds and then to the hill that seemed to tower over them like a giant. It looked so serene, so quiet and safe. But at any moment it could buckle....A shiver of fear moved up her spine, and she stiffened. Dominic offered his hand as they climbed onto the green concrete foundation at the bottom of the cofferdam.

"You're doing fine," he whispered encouragingly, placing his arm protectively about her waist as they threaded around the rebar that stuck up like pins in a cushion.

A suffocating feeling washed over her, and she wanted to shriek. The PZ-38 sheeting seemed to close in like corrugated monsters ready to pounce upon them. Miserably she shook her head, stumbling. No, she couldn't let her wild imagination destroy what they had just discovered in each other. There was no way she could allow it to destroy her burgeoning love for Dominic.

"Look out!" a voice screamed far above them.

Cait gasped as Dominic wrenched her off her feet, pushing her heavily against the wall. There was a shearing sound intermingled with more warning cries, and suddenly the cofferdam quivered as tons of muddy earth slid into its mouth.

She whimpered softly, clinging to Dominic as he

lifted her away from the wall, nearly carrying her toward the shore wall. Wildly she looked to the right—mud slithered like a huge boa constrictor into the bottom of the cofferdam, released from the failing upper-retaining wall. He breathed in harshly. "Are you all right?"

Cait nodded numbly, her skin pulled taut across her cheekbones.

"Dolph!" he roared. He hoisted Cait above his head, toward outstretched hands. "Get her out of here! Now!"

She started to struggle, but the German's meaty hands hooked her beneath each armpit, and she was suddenly pulled clear of the cofferdam. She had lost her hard hat, and the rain plastered her dark hair against her frozen face as she stared down at the lone figure in the bottom of that hungry, insatiable monster.

She heard Dominic roaring a series of orders that sent men and machines scurrying like ants into the breach in the upper retaining wall. She stumbled backward, her hands across her mouth. She wanted to escape, to run away. But Dominic intended to stay there. He wasn't afraid. He knew what he was doing.

Suddenly the strangling cape of fear slid off her shoulders, and she was able to take in a full breath of air. Shakily she pushed the wet hair off her face, feeling her muddy fingers streak her skin, but not caring. She saw Dominic twist around, a grin on his face. He waved confidently to her and then returned to directing the men with shovels and buckets. The rain was easing now to a light sprinkle, and she turned away from the cofferdam, slowly trudging through the ankle-deep mud in an easterly direction, toward Bahia Linda. . . .

By the time she found what was left of the path, the murky skies were breaking up in jigsaw-shaped clouds. The biting wind turned to a gentle breeze, and she took another deep, calming breath.

Despite the ravages of the torrential rains and the debris carried by the Rio Colorado, the small bay was untouched by the storm. Here and there, gray horneros flitted from one cypress tree to another, calling for their mates. Cait made her way down the narrow trail, her rubber boots making prints in the black sand as she traversed the beach to a moss-covered log at the other end of the cove. Miraculously the blue water of the lagoon remained clear of silt.

Sitting down, Cait rested her hand against her forehead, shutting her eyes tightly. Soon the sounds of peace chased away her anxiety, and she relaxed.

Her mind cartwheeled over a hundred facets of her relationship with Dominic. Had it only been a few months since she had fallen so helplessly in love with him? Where had it all begun? How had love reawakened her grieving heart and coaxed new life into it?

She thought of Dave, and for the first time there was no answering squeeze of pain. Dominic had been right—with time, the pain would leave completely, and only the warmth of good memories would remain.

She picked up a broken twig that had been torn loose in the wind. She had been like that twig—torn loose from its steady mooring in a happy marriage and cast helplessly adrift. Yet meeting Dominic had changed all that.

She looked up, watching the churning clouds part to allow a weak stream of sunlight to touch the jungle across the river. Dominic had been a light to her, helping her to realize that love did not die, that it was possible to continue living and loving.

A soft smile touched her haggard features as she stared down at the twig. Yes, love had shown both of them that it was possible to hope... to laugh... and to share the good and bad times—together. She had confronted her worst fear—losing him—and she had won. Their love had been tested early, and had held fast.

Cait was unaware of Dominic's presence until she heard the soft snap of a water-soaked branch beneath his foot as he approached. She jerked her head up, watching him walk slowly across the beach. Her heart skyrocketed and she sat up straighter, clutching at the twig in her hand as he halted a few feet from her. He was splattered with mud, and his hard hat dangled limply in his left hand as he caught and held her questioning gaze.

Another sensation squeezed her heart when she realized he had gone without rest for almost forty hours. The enormity of his physical endurance shook her as her eyes scanned the deep lines at the corners of his eyes and mouth. Three days' growth of beard made his features gaunt, and the rain-soaked clothing rounded out his disheveled form.

He rested on one leg, one hand on his hip. "I thought I might find you here," he said. "Is there room for one more on that log? I don't think I can stand up much longer."

She moved over. "You look awful."

"You never looked lovelier," he answered huskily. "The cofferdam—"

"Minor landslide. The tie-backs are holding. It was just a matter of shoveling the mud out of the floor. I've got the bulldozers scraping about eight feet of soil off the crest. The sun's coming out." He sighed, resting his arms heavily on his thighs. "It'll dry up in a day or two and we can replace those tie-back cables and it will be like nothing ever happened." He turned, drinking in her weary face. "Something did happen, though."

She nodded tiredly, resting her forehead against his broad shoulder. "Too much," she agreed. His arm slid around her waist, drawing her close.

"I was damn proud of you, Cait. I was betting everything on you coming with me . . . and you did. God, I love you so much. I know how much courage it took to go down in there with me." He touched her chin, forcing her to meet his golden eyes. "I saw the pain and fear in your face, querida. It had to be done. You realize that, don't you?"

Hot tears slid from her eyes, and she tasted their saltiness as they ran into the corners of her trembling parted lips. "Yes. But nature didn't have to emphasize the point by providing a landslide just then!"

He laughed, lifting her to her feet and hugging her tightly. "Mi leona . . . I named you well," he said, kissing her cheek and holding her at arm's length. He brushed away a smudge of mud from her forehead, a gentle smile playing on his mouth. "I saw your courage and conviction the first day I met you, and as I got to know more about you, I admired your strength. It took me ten years after a broken, ugly marriage to even lift my head up and look around. You were doing it in a year's time." His eyes narrowed, his voice husky with emotion. "How much you've taught me, Cait. . . . How much more we can share and give to each other from this day forward."

A muffled cry broke from her lips as she sought his warming embrace. They stood there a long, long time, leaning silently against each other, their hearts pounding to the other's soothing rhythm. Cait nuzzled his neck, inhaling the male odor that was him. It was a perfume to her heightened senses.

"I thought," she began, "that if I couldn't conquer my fear of your being injured—or killed—that I didn't love you enough..." Her voice cracked and she choked back a sob.

"That's ridiculous," he chided huskily, placing light kisses over her cheek and forehead. "I would love you just as much now even if you hadn't gone down there with me." He touched her hair. "Never question your love for me, querida, or mine for you. It's strong and good." A subdued amber light flickered to life in his eyes as he cupped her face in his large hands. "Now, will you tell me you love me? It's all I'll ever need to hear."

She leaned upward, her lips meeting his mobile, generous mouth in a kiss that dazzled her senses. How long she remained wrapped in his arms, she did not know. Finally he dragged his mouth from hers and she murmured huskily, "I love you."

They sauntered up the trail toward the crest where Bahia Linda began. Once on top, Dominic pointed to the Rio Colorado. The gray sky was parting, and strong shafts of late-afternoon sunlight pierced the thinning clouds, turning the iron-colored mud into brilliant crimson, and the tropical plants into a lush green. He leaned over, whispering in her ear, "That's for us. A bright new beginning, querida. A promise of a life to come that will hold sunshine and laughter even in the bad times. We'll tackle every storm together, and our love will see us through it."

There's nothing more precious than your

Second Chance at Love
™

All of the above titles are $1.75 per copy

Second Chance at Love

All of the above titles are $1.75 per copy